Bofuri

, so
e.

M000158679

KASUMI

Kasumi's STATS

Lv58
HP 435/435
MP 70/70
[STR 170]
[VIT 80]
[AGI 90]
[DEX 30]
[INT 20]

Welcome to
NewWorld Online.

"Break Core!"

This skill was fundamentally a self-destruct technique.

A moment later, a pillar of flames pierced the heavens, consuming Maple with it.

Fighting the strongest on the fourth stratum.

Bofuri

I Don't Want to Get Hurt, so I'll Max Out My Defense.

⑤

YUUMIKAN

Illustration by KOIN

YEN ON
NEW YORK

Welcome to
NewWorld Online.

Bofuri I Don't Want to Get Hurt, so I'll Max Out My Defense.

YUUMIKAN

Translation by Andrew Cunningham • Cover art by KOIN

This book is a work of fiction. Names, characters, places, and incidents are the product of the author's imagination or are used fictitiously. Any resemblance to actual events, locales, or persons, living or dead, is coincidental.

ITAINO WA IYA NANODE BOGYORYOKU NI KYOKUFURI SHITAITO OMOIMASU. Vol. 5
©Yuumikan, Koin 2018
First published in Japan in 2018 by KADOKAWA CORPORATION, Tokyo.
English translation rights arranged with KADOKAWA CORPORATION, Tokyo, through TUTTLE-MORI AGENCY, INC., Tokyo.

English translation © 2022 by Yen Press, LLC

Yen On
150 West 30th Street, 19th Floor
New York, NY 10001

Visit us at yenpress.com • facebook.com/yenpress
yenpress.tumblr.com • instagram.com/yenpress

First Yen On Edition: April 2022

Yen On is an imprint of Yen Press, LLC.
The Yen On name and logo are trademarks of Yen Press, LLC.

The publisher is not responsible for websites (or their content) that are not owned by the publisher.

Library of Congress Cataloging-in-Publication Data
Names: Yuumikan, author. | Koin, illustrator. | Cunningham, Andrew, 1979– translator.
Title: Bofuri, I don't want to get hurt, so I'll max out my defense / Yuumikan ; illustration by Koin ; translated by Andrew Cunningham.
Other titles: Itai no wa iya nano de bōgyoryoku ni kyokufuri shitai to omoimasu. English
Description: First Yen On edition. | New York : Yen On, 2021–
Identifiers: LCCN 2020055872 | ISBN 9781975322731 (v. 1 ; trade paperback) |
    ISBN 9781975323547 (v. 2 ; trade paperback) | ISBN 9781975323561 (v. 3 ; trade paperback) |
    ISBN 9781975323585 (v. 4 ; trade paperback) | ISBN 9781975323608 (v. 5 ; trade paperback)
Subjects: LCSH: Video gamers—Fiction. | Virtual reality—Fiction. | GSAFD: Science fiction.
Classification: LCC PL874.I46 I8313 2021 | DDC 895.63/6—dc23
LC record available at https://lccn.loc.gov/2020055872

ISBNs: 978-1-9753-2360-8 (paperback)
       978-1-9753-2361-5 (ebook)

10 9 8 7 6 5 4 3 2 1

LSC-C

Printed in the United States of America

CONTENTS

I Don't Want to Get Hurt,
so I'll Max Out My Defense.

NewWorld Online Status

||NAME Maple ||Maple LV **40**

HP 200/200 MP 22/22

STATUS

[STR] 000 [VIT] 8880 [AGI] 000 [DEX] 000 [INT] 000

EQUIPMENT

|| New Moon: Hydra || Night's Facsimile: Devour || Bonding Bridge

|| Black Rose Armor: Saturating Chaos || Toughness Ring || Life Ring

SKILLS

Shield Attack   Sidestep   Deflect   Meditation   Taunt   Inspire   HP Boost (S)   MP Boost (S)

Great Shield Mastery V   Cover Move IV   Cover   Pierce Guard   Counter   Absolute Defense

Moral Turpitude   Giant Killing   Hydra Eater   Bomb Eater   Sheep Eater   Indomitable Guardian

Psychokinesis   Fortress   Martyr's Devotion   Machine God

NewWorld Online Status

||NAME Sally ||Sally LV **37**

HP 32/32 MP 80/80

STATUS

[STR] 085 [VIT] 000 [AGI] 158 [DEX] 045 [INT] 050

EQUIPMENT

|| Deep Sea Dagger || Seabed Dagger

|| Surface Scarf: Mirage || Oceanic Coat: Oceanic

|| Oceanic Clothes || Black Boots || Bonding Bridge

SKILLS

Gale Slash   Defense Break   Inspire   Down Attack   Power Attack   Switch Attack

Combo Blade V   Martial Arts V   Fire Magic II   Water Magic III   Wind Magic III   Earth Magic II

Dark Magic II   Light Magic II   Strength Boost (S)   Combo Boost (S)   MP Boost (S)   MP Cost Down (S)

MP Recovery Speed Boost (S)   Poison Resist (S)   Gathering Speed Boost (S)   Dagger Mastery VI

Magic Mastery III   Affliction VI   Presence Block II   Presence Detect II   Sneaky Steps I   Leap III

Cooking I   Fishing   Swimming X   Diving X   Shearing   Superspeed   Ancient Ocean

Chaser Blade   Jack of All Trades   Sword Dance

I Don't Want to Get Hurt, so I'll Max Out My Defense

Welcome to NewWorld Online

‖ NAME Chrome **HP** 840/840 **MP** 52/52 **LV** 61

STATUS

⟦STR⟧ 130 ⟦VIT⟧ 175 ⟦AGI⟧ 020 ⟦DEX⟧ 030 ⟦INT⟧ 010

EQUIPMENT

‖ Headhunter: Life Eater   ‖ Wrath Wraith Wall: Soul Syphon

‖ Bloodstained Skull: Soul Eater   ‖ Bloodstained Bone Armor: Dead or Alive

‖ Robust Ring   ‖ Impregnable Ring   ‖ Defense Ring

SKILLS

Thrust   Flame Slash   Ice Blade   Shield Attack   Sidestep   Deflect   Great Defense
Taunt   Impregnable Stance   HP Boost (L)   HP Recovery Speed Boost (L)   MP Boost (S)
Great Shield Mastery X   Defense Mastery X   Cover Move X   Cover   Pierce Guard   Counter   Guard Aura
Defensive Formation   Guardian Power   Great Shield Secrets III   Defense Secrets II   Poison Nullification
Paralyze Nullification   Stun Resist (L)   Sleep Resist (L)   Freeze Nullification   Burn Resist (L)
Mining IV   Gathering V   Shearing   Spirit Light   Indomitable Guardian   Battle Healing

‖ NAME Iz **HP** 100/100 **MP** 100/100 **LV** 44

STATUS

⟦STR⟧ 045 ⟦VIT⟧ 020 ⟦AGI⟧ 075 ⟦DEX⟧ 210 ⟦INT⟧ 030

EQUIPMENT

‖ Blacksmith Hammer X   ‖ Alchemist Goggles: Faustian Alchemy

‖ Alchemist Long Coat: Magic Workshop   ‖ Blacksmith Leggings X

‖ Alchemist Boots: New Frontier   ‖ Potion Pouch   ‖ Item Pouch   ‖ Black Gloves

SKILLS

Strike   Crafting Mastery X   Crafting Secrets II   Enhance Success Rate Boost (L)
Gathering Speed Boost (L)   Mining Speed Boost (L)   Affliction II   Sneaky Steps III   Smithing X
Sewing X   Horticulture X   Synthesizing X   Augmentation X   Cooking X   Mining X   Gathering X
Swimming IV   Diving V   Shearing   Godsmith's Grace IX

‖ NAME Kanade **HP** 335/335 **MP** 290/290 **LV** 30

STATUS

⟦STR⟧ 015 ⟦VIT⟧ 010 ⟦AGI⟧ 040 ⟦DEX⟧ 035 ⟦INT⟧ 110

EQUIPMENT

‖ Divine Wisdom: Akashic Records   ‖ Diamond Newsboy Cap VIII

‖ Smart Coat VI   ‖ Smart Leggings VIII   ‖ Smart Boots VI

‖ Spade Earrings   ‖ Mage Gloves   ‖ Holy Ring

SKILLS

Magic Mastery VI   MP Boost (M)   MP Cost Down (S)   MP Recovery Speed Boost (M)
Magic Boost (S)   Fire Magic IV   Water Magic III   Wind Magic IV   Earth Magic II   Dark Magic II
Light Magic III   Sorcerer's Stacks

NAME Kasumi | HP 435/435 | MP 70/70 | **LV 58**

STATUS
[STR] 170 [VIT] 080 [AGI] 090 [DEX] 030 [INT] 020

EQUIPMENT
Unsigned Katana	Cherry Blossom Barrette	Cherry Blossom Vestments
Edo Purple Hakama	Samurai Greaves	Samurai Gauntlets
Gold Obi Fastener	Cherry Blossom Crest

SKILLS
Gleam · Helmsplitter · Guard Break · Sweep Slice · Eye for Attack · Inspire · Attack Stance · Katana Arts X · Cleave · Throw · HP Boost (L) · MP Boost (M) · Poison Nullification · Paralyze Nullification · Stun Resist (M) · Sleep Resist (M) · Freeze Resist (S) · Burn Resist (S) · Longsword Mastery X · Katana Mastery X · Longsword Secrets II · Katana Secrets II · Mining IV · Gathering VI · Diving V · Swimming VI · Leap VII · Shearing · Keen Sight · Indomitable · Sword Spirit · Dauntless · Sinew · Superspeed · Ever Vigilant

---

NAME Mai | HP 35/35 | MP 20/20 | **LV 28**

STATUS
[STR] 325 [VIT] 000 [AGI] 000 [DEX] 000 [INT] 000

EQUIPMENT
| Black Annihilammer VIII | Black Doll Dress VIII | Black Doll Tights VIII |
| Black Doll Shoes VIII | Little Ribbon | Silk Gloves |

SKILLS
Double Stamp · Double Impact · Double Strike · Attack Boost (S) · Hammer Mastery IV · Throw · Farshot · Conqueror · Annihilator · Giant Killing

---

NAME Yui | HP 35/35 | MP 20/20 | **LV 28**

STATUS
[STR] 325 [VIT] 000 [AGI] 000 [DEX] 000 [INT] 000

EQUIPMENT
| White Annihilammer VIII | White Doll Dress VIII | White Doll Tights VIII |
| White Doll Shoes VIII | Little Ribbon | Silk Gloves |

SKILLS
Double Stamp · Double Impact · Double Strike · Attack Boost (S) · Hammer Mastery II · Throw · Farshot · Conqueror · Annihilator · Giant Killing

Maple's tactic of raising only defense had left her far more OP than she ever expected to be. She founded a small (but elite) guild named Maple Tree and, together with her newfound friends, beat the odds to place third in the guild wars event. Their reward: contact with top players in other guilds and access permits usable only on the fourth stratum—which had yet to launch.

A month after the event, a day in early October...

This was the day *NewWorld Online* finally launched the fourth stratum.

Like everyone else, Maple had been looking forward to it. She would have logged in right after the update maintenance was finished even if Sally hadn't suggested it first.

Maple arrived at their Guild Home and immediately started looking for Sally. She found her on the couch in the back, waving.

"I'm here!" Maple said. "What now? Take a run at it?"

"Pretty sure you're all we need to take the third-stratum boss, so why not? You're already dying to see it, aren't you?"

"Yesssss!"

It seemed like Sally hadn't invited any other guild members. It was just the two of them.

Even if they went up a stratum now, they'd likely have to fight the boss again when the rest of the guild was ready to push on. Maple Tree might have been one of the best guilds on the server, but without their top two fighters, success invariably became a lot less certain.

Maple and Sally knew that—but neither of them could resist the temptation to check out the next map.

Sally didn't even bother confirming what the new boss was. She just had Maple enter Atrocity mode and rode her across the field before proceeding directly into the dungeon.

Maple was unquestionably famous by now, so players on their flying machines no longer mistook her inhuman form for a monster. And of course, nobody was stupid enough to attack her.

That didn't stop them from staring a lot, though.

Trampling the dungeon monsters underfoot, Maple brought them straight to the boss room.

"Sally! We're here!"

"Cool! This shouldn't take long."

Maple used her monster limbs to pry open the door. Inside, they found giant steel golems three times taller than the both of them put together.

If the golems had been sentient, they probably would have taken one look at the hideous monsters peering through the crack in the doorway and gone white as a sheet.

Instead, they just got ready to attack.

Sally took one look at them and busted out a big move.

"Oboro! Phantom World!"

*   *   *

This spell had come in handy during the fourth event. For three full minutes, it created three autonomous clones of the spell's target—with identical stats.

In other words, Sally had just told her pet monster, Oboro, to give them *four* Maples.

Each of the Maples threw themselves at a golem, practically coiling around their victims.

The golems fought back, but Maple's defense was nearing five figures, and she took no damage.

Sally relaxed and sat down to play with Oboro.

But a few minutes later, Maple let out a cry of alarm.

"Sally! What do I do?!"

"Maple?! What's wrong?!"

"I can't hurt them!"

"You can't?!"

Sally took another look. The golems were all at full HP.

The admins had been *thinking.*

At last, they had come up with a way to nerf Maple's Atrocity without simultaneously ruining everyone else's day.

Instead of dropping an unreasonably strong boss like Silver Wings, they'd simply made one with high defense and lots of HP.

Maple was thwarted not by a foe that could hurt her—but one with the *same build.*

After all, she didn't have any armor-piercing attacks.

Her primary damage dealer was poison, but if her opponent could resist that…she didn't have many other options.

The golems couldn't hurt Maple, but she couldn't hurt them, either.

The admins had finally figured out a way to stop Maple from soloing everything.

"I guess this one's mine, then," Sally said, drawing her daggers. She broke into a run.

Half an hour later...

Sally had maxed out the attack boost Sword Dance provided, and the battle finally drew to a close.

"Hmm, maybe I need better ways to deal with tanks..."

"That...was pretty tough."

Their plan to overwhelm the boss and rush onto the fourth stratum had certainly not gone as expected, but the task was done. It was time to collect their drops and head on up.

"What do you think it's like?"

"Good question. Look, we're almost there."

Sally ran out ahead, and Maple did her best to follow.

The fourth stratum was home to a town of everlasting night.

Two full moons hung in the star-studded sky—one blue, one red.

This was clearly the biggest town they'd seen yet. All the buildings were made of wood, giving it that ye-olde-Japan feel.

Canals ran through the town, and lanterns lit the paths.

Standing at the heart of everything was a tantalizingly tall tower, calling to them.

"Wanna explore? Like, right now?"

"Sure. But first, we should stop by our Guild Home," Sally suggested.

"Whoops, good point."

Guild Homes allowed access to the guild's communal storage on any stratum, and a single visit on a new map allowed

members to warp to that town as well as to their Guild Home on that stratum.

Invariably, it was the first place everybody went on every new stratum.

Maple and Sally hurried toward it, resisting the siren call of adventure.

CHAPTER 1

Defense Build and the Town of Ever-Night

Once they'd located their Guild Home, they went inside, scoping out the interior. There were tatami floors in the private rooms, and the common space had nothing in it but a sunken hearth and charcoal stove. A good match for the fourth stratum's traditional Japanese vibe.

As they finished exploring for the moment, Sally noticed the rest of their guild had logged in.

"Hey, Maple, looks like everyone's online."

"Should we go help? I can't do much but keep them safe with Martyr's Devotion, but..."

"That's more than enough! C'mon."

Deciding that further exploration could wait, they flitted back down to the stratum below.

With Maple's angel form keeping them safe from harm, Mai and Yui's barrage of piercing attacks made shockingly short work of the boss fight.

"I...should have known we'd be useless..."

"Do what I do, Chrome," Kasumi said, also idly watching the golems go down. "Tell yourself you're conserving energy for exploring the new map."

"There'll be new materials to check out. Can't wait," Iz said. "Hopefully the monsters aren't *too* tough."

"I could help with that. More than I am here, anyway...," Kanade said, putting his Rubik's Cube away.

"I'll take you up on that."

The four spectators knew how full-guild boss fights worked by this point. As soon as the short fight was over, Maple waved them onward, eager to explore, and they all fell in behind her.

As they set foot on the new stratum, Maple Tree's members went their separate ways, everyone exploring for themselves.

The plan was to report back later, share information, and learn the lay of the land in this new town.

◆□◆□◆□◆□◆

Maple was on her own, head swiveling this way and that as all the new sights and sounds fought for her attention.

One road led her to a red torii gate with a sign on it displaying only a ceremonial kanji for the number one.

When she tried to pass through it, a voice demanded her access permit.

"Um...I'm allowed in, right?"

She slowly stretched a foot forward and, when nothing happened, hopped across the threshold.

"Oh! That's right, I *do* have a permit. How far does it go, again?"

After remembering that ranking in the last event had given her surprisingly far-reaching access privileges, Maple continued on her merry way.

This was how the fourth stratum was structured. Approaching the center of town required access permits for the torii gates.

Players without any permits would have to complete quests before they could progress further. Exploring right away was a luxury reserved for the champions.

And the farther in you went, the higher the odds of finding good equipment and skills.

For a fee, NPCs would carry you via gondola or rickshaw to preset locations. Maple decided to board one of the latter shortly after crossing a gate with the ceremonial kanji for two. She did still have a lot of ground to cover, but mostly, she just wanted to ride one.

"So fast! And the breeze feels great!"

It was infinitely faster than Maple's walking speed, swiftly hauling her deeper into town.

When she disembarked, she found herself outside the gate marked Six.

She tried stepping through, but a wall of pale light suddenly appeared and barred her path. Maple's access permit had the kanji for five on it, and evidently, she could progress no further.

"Aw…that tower's still a long way off. I wonder how you raise your access rank?"

Maple gave up on moving forward for the moment and ducked into a nearby shop.

"Hellooo…oh wow, there are so many kimonos!"

Everything inside looked like something Kasumi would wear.

"I guess these clothes are a better fit for this town…"

Maple decided to change her outfit. She could easily change it again if she got in a fight, so she unequipped her shield and short sword, switching to tourist mode.

She picked a purple kimono—matching her Hydra's poison—and left the shop wearing it.

"Where to next?" she said, looking *very* pleased with herself.

"Next" proved to be a shop filled with furniture and home goods.

A male NPC was seated at the back—the shop's owner.

Inside, there were old vases, hanging scrolls, and low tables as far as the eye could see.

Everything here could be used to decorate their Guild Home.

"Are these supposed to be super fancy or something? They're definitely expensive, but...I don't really know."

Maple looked over the wares, but lacking an eye for antiquities, she soon gave up and turned to go.

Then the old owner called out to her. "Little lady, won't you have a look at this urn before you go?"

"Me? Hmm...I dunno..."

Urns didn't exactly get Maple's heart racing, but if he'd gone to the trouble to pick it out for her... She decided it was safer to take a look. Better than wondering *what if* later.

"Over here..."

The owner opened a door in the back, beckoning her into a room with nothing on display.

Maple followed and spotted an urn with a lid, one small enough to fit on the palm of her hand.

"Is this it? Hmm...yeah, not really my style."

But then a blue screen appeared in the air in front of her.

"Huh? A quest?!"

That changed everything.

Most quests came with minimum stat requirements, and since Maple had only raised defense, she didn't get to do many. She wasn't about to blow this rare chance.

She hit the ACCEPT button so fast she didn't even have time to read the screen.

"Good! Try to be the last survivor," the owner said—and removed the lid.

Maple was instantly sucked into the urn.

"Wait, whaaat?!"

Maple tried to recall her brief glimpse of the quest title but drew a blank.

She had no idea it was called The Urn-King.

For a moment, Maple was in the air…then she landed hard on her butt.

"Owww! Wh-where am I?"

She looked around.

It was dark, and the ground was flat. In the distance, she could see tall, curved walls made of…something inorganic. It was too dark to see the top, so all she could tell was that it continued way up; there was no sign of an exit.

And the zone itself was so big, she felt reluctant to walk the entire length of it.

"…Something's coming closer?"

Maple put a hand to her brow, squinting. She could make out solid-looking purple scorpions and centipedes in the distance. There were even some spiders with what seemed like thick carapaces. And they were all scuttling toward her.

And moving quickly, to boot—they were already looking much bigger than when she'd first spotted them.

"Aha! So I just have to beat all of them. I get it now!"

She quickly reached for the sword at her hip.

"Eep?! Wh-where is it?!"

She had still been in tourist mode when the battle started, meaning her shield and weapon were both currently stowed away in her inventory.

"Uh-oh…uh, uh…"

She quickly tapped the air, pulling up the menu.

But she was in such a rush, she accidentally hit the wrong item, and the lost time that blunder cost her only made her panic harder. The fastest scorpion had Maple trapped in its pincers before she could hit the EQUIPMENT CHANGE button.

"No, don't! Not yet! Time-out!"

Now involuntarily airborne, she was trapped—but the monster's attacks also didn't hurt her. The pincers ground against her sides, and the scorpion slammed its poison stinger into Maple, but to no avail. Regardless, none of this was helping her calm down.

"Stop! Put me down! I dunno what to do!"

Maple herself was fine…but her brand-new kimono was not so lucky.

"You're ripping it! Aw…blegh! Don't drip nasty poison on me!"

A centipede had reared itself up and was hovering above her, dripping purple goo all over her—which did absolutely nothing to Maple.

But it was definitely messing up her equipment.

She tried again to swap gear, but before she could, her kimono shattered in a shower of light. It had never been designed to be worn in battle.

"Aw…"

Maple quit struggling, letting her legs dangle limply. Her cheeks puffed up as she started sulking. There was no longer any need to change gear fast, so she took her time, letting the noxious gunk drip off her.

Back in her all-black gear, she twisted her shield as far as it would go, tapping it on the scorpion's claw. At last, she was finally free.

"Wow, there's a *lot* of them," Maple muttered. Another spurt of purple gunk splattered on her head.

They'd crowded in while she was trapped. Everywhere she looked, there were monsters—and most of them were poisonous.

"Argh, I'm gonna exterminate all of you!"

Mourning the loss of her kimono, Maple summoned her Predators, then used Martyr's Devotion.

"Full Deploy!"

There was a metallic *clunk*, and Maple bristled with the Machine God's armaments.

"Commence Assault!"

Artillery fire rained down on the monsters...and bounced right off their thick shells.

"Wha—?! ...Is magic the only way to hurt them? But I bet poison would be even more useless against these guys..."

All of these monsters had purple shells. Even things that usually didn't have shells, like the snakes! Maple looked around and made a face.

"They all look tanky. That's gonna be a pain!"

Maple's attacks—and those of her Predators—mostly landed on the scorpion closest to her.

That flurry of hits cracked the carapace, exposing the soft flesh underneath.

"Oh, good! That got through faster than I expected. Saturating Chaos!"

Maple unleashed a monstrous maw that turned the scorpion into a spray of light.

The monsters didn't seem to have much HP, but they made up for it in numbers.

And her Predators were coming under constant attack, so this was going to take a while.

"Oh!" Maple said. "First, let me put the Predators away…"

When they were gone, she aimed all her gun barrels at the ground, rocketing skyward.

"Syrup!"

She summoned her pet in midair and promptly Giganticized it.

Then she had it hover below her and dropped it down onto its back.

"Eh-heh-heh! Thanks, Syrup."

She patted its shell, then gave the next order.

"Um, open wide?"

Obediently, Syrup opened its mouth, and Maple put her feet inside. It wound up holding her by the knees.

"Good, good."

Syrup had been flying straight and level, but now she had it hover at an angle so that they were perpendicular to the ground.

With Maple still dangling from Syrup's mouth, all her artillery barrels were now aimed directly at the ground.

"Commence Assault! First, I've gotta crack their shells."

Lasers and bullets rained down from above.

"I feel like a crane game…"

Maple used her Psychokinesis to move Syrup in circles around the field, carpet-bombing everything below.

She had a good view of the ground and could easily tell if the monster shells were cracked or not; she kept moving and kept firing.

"All righty… Now I just have to drop down and finish them off!"

There was no more need for her to stay floating, so she put Syrup back in her ring, flipped through the air, and landed feetfirst.

"Time to mop up! Here I come!"

The only response was the sound of monsters screaming as they exploded into showers of light.

With the shells gone, Maple could easily damage these monsters.

And since none of them could hurt her, she handily wiped the floor with them.

"Okay! Last one!"

When her final bullet struck home, the world instantly went black—and then she found herself back in the shop.

"The owner's gone? Whoa!"

The *Quest Complete* panel had just popped up.

It gave her a new skill.

"Bug Urn Curse? What is *that*?"

Bug Urn Curse

Applies a 10% instant death chance to all poison attacks. This is unaffected by poison resistance skills.

"Oh...oh? Wait a minute... That means it ignores Poison Nullification, right?"

There had been a noticeable uptick in players and monsters with Poison Resist or Poison Nullification, which had made Hydra a lot less useful, but this Bug Urn Curse gave her a chance to one-shot those players. Poison Nullification no longer guaranteed their safety.

"I'll have to try it out soon. But for now..."

Maple left the deserted shop and dragged her feet over to another.

"Ugh, I gotta buy it *again*..."

Mourning the death of her kimono, she purchased another identical one.

"Well, I'm just going to enjoy the hell out of *this* one!"

She decided the sacrifice had been worth the skill she'd learned and headed back out dressed to the nines once again.

CHAPTER 2

Defense Build and Kasumi

A few days after the fourth stratum opened…

The guild members had completed the initial exploration and gathered at their home to report the results.

"I've been doing some leveling and a few quests," Chrome began. "I mostly hit up the fields outside of town. Lots of yokai-looking monsters. Feels like more monsters that cast magic in general."

Iz nodded, adding, "I was also out there gathering materials. Honestly, it's pretty rough going without someone to fight for me."

"I took the twins and went one gate at a time," Kanade said. "I figured the rest of you would skip over those areas, but they've got plenty of quests and shops with materials you can't buy farther in. Here's the data…"

He passed out files with the full breakdown.

"Yui and I explored some, but the place is so big!"

"Definitely the biggest one yet."

They both shared what they'd found. But every member was stuck at the same torii gate.

"And you, Maple?" Sally said.

"I bought a kimono and got an instant death skill!"

"......Ooookay, we'll need the full version of that later." That small snippet was more than enough to safely assume Maple had done something outrageous again, so Sally decided now wasn't the time for a deep dive. "But one thing's clear—we all got pretty far in."

Her comment was about the access permits.

Without one of those, players could barely do anything on this stratum.

Going farther into town required completing quests to raise your access rank, and they were all fairly intense.

Chrome and Kasumi had clearly figured that out, but Maple was never one to actively pursue this type of information. It was news to her.

"Then our access is, like, amazing?"

"It's certainly a big advantage."

They were allowed to skip right past a number of barriers blocking the average player's progress.

For a while, the conversation focused on what quests could be found where, but nobody else seemed interested in trying Maple's quest.

"Well, send a message if anything comes up!" Maple said, sending everyone on their separate ways.

They were all exploring, but the fourth stratum's town was so much bigger than any previous areas that it was starting to feel endless.

One afternoon several days later...

Maple was taking a break at the Guild Home, sipping some tea Iz had made.

"Well? Enjoying the town?"

"It's...big."

"I've found some interesting materials, but...some of them are only available in *one* shop, so my overall progress has been pretty slow."

With Maple Tree's access level, all of them could go pretty far in—but there was plenty to discover in the outer areas, not to mention the fields outside of town.

Even just gathering materials was quite a bit more involved than any previous map.

"I've learned how to make some new items. Not enough materials to mass-produce anything yet, but they should come in handy in due time."

"Nice!"

At this point, the front door opened, letting Chrome, Mai, and Yui come in.

"Oh, Iz! Perfect. I gathered some mats for you while finishing up that quest."

"Thanks," she said, grinning. "Well? Want a drink? Some of these are new on this level."

"...This floor's materials have some dubious names, so I think I'll pass."

Chrome had spotted a smirk behind Iz's grin and quickly decided he'd stick to coffee. Mai and Yui ordered cocoa. Everyone joined Maple at the table.

"Whew... So, Maple, any luck in your travels?"

"This place is *so* big! I've been running all over."

The twins nodded sympathetically.

"We basically live on rickshaws now."

"It's expensive but way, way faster than walking!"

"There are *so many* quests. And shops. They're mostly selling decorative stuff, though... Still, always worth a look."

"All that expensive furniture... I think I'm good just window shopping."

"Some of these quests require you to drop money on 'em, too. How and when are we supposed to afford anything extra?"

Maple had been in all kinds of shops but only bought consumable items.

"We've got rooms here, so I'd like to decorate a *bit*."

The Guild Home had a private room for each of them. Maple didn't like leaving hers empty, so she'd bought something for it on each stratum.

As they talked, Sally and Kanade joined them, and Kasumi later emerged from her room.

"Oh, we're all here now!"

"Was that planned?"

Maple told Sally what they'd been chatting about so far.

"I really haven't done much," Sally said. "Just checked out some new items and poked my nose in a few promising corners of the field while I was out questing."

"My only real find is a shop selling wooden puzzles. Good ones. Lemme know if you wanna borrow any."

Kanade had already completed all of them and was currently pestering Iz to make him something harder.

"But there's still tons of town to explore. If I see anything you'll like, Maple, I'll make a mental note of it."

"Great, thanks!"

"It's not all combat-oriented stuff, either. I think...you might enjoy the shops around here," Kasumi said, opening her map and pointing to a few locations.

"Oooh, I see... I'll check it out. You know a lot, Kasumi!"

"Mm? Uh, yeah... Just lucky, I suppose," she replied, quickly putting the map away.

Iz and Kanade finished conferring, and she offered drinks again.

"Nah, better not. I'm heading straight to the fields."

"Okay. Careful…and good luck."

Everyone watched Kasumi go, then Maple frowned.

"She's been visiting the field a lot lately," she said.

"Maybe she's just low on cash like the rest of us?"

"Yeah…we're so broke…"

The twins' theory made a lot of sense to Maple.

"…Considering how much grinding she's done, I doubt that…"

Iz had a much firmer grasp on the prices of materials and items, but then Kanade's puzzles came to mind and promptly pushed everything else out of her thoughts.

"Either way, Kasumi's not the type to do anything stupid, and I've gotta get crafting!"

"Oh, you're starting on my order already? Make it a really hard one, please."

And once again, everyone went their separate ways, enjoying the new stratum on their own terms.

Kasumi sneaked back in late that night when she was sure her guildmates had long since finished playing for the day. Once the door to her private room closed behind her, she let out a sigh.

"…This is heaven…"

Her room was filled with row after row of purchases she'd made the last few days.

Pottery that caught her eye, swords she had no intention of ever taking into battle, and everything in between.

Unlike in the real world, being broke in *NWO* just meant you had to go kill some monsters. A few shopping sprees never hurt anyone.

But perhaps Kasumi had taken things a little too far.

"Just one more run to the store...! Then I'll have to go earn a bit more."

The gold listed on her stat menu was getting worryingly low.

And what she was after was hardly cheap. Her tastes ran on the pricey side.

But she had never had so much fun.

"I'll go farther in than anyone else! Heh-heh..."

She glanced down at her access permit. Without telling the others, she'd raised it to six.

What treasures lay within that untouched zone?

"Let's find out! Time's a-wasting!"

She put the permit back in her inventory and flew out of the Guild Home.

◆□◆□◆□◆□◆

Ten days later, Kasumi was in her room again, staring at her stat screen.

Specifically, at one corner of it.

"Urp..."

Kasumi had been gradually saving up money all this time, having found no real use for it—but now she'd blown all her savings on random things that didn't even affect her stats.

The total amount: five times the gold required to found Maple Tree itself.

Each torii gate a player passed through brought them ever closer to the heart of the town. Despite the clear partitioning, the whole place was so massive that each area took ages to explore.

Even so, Kasumi had been to every single antique shop.

The time she had spent gazing at all the merchandise had been the purest bliss.

And her passion for it had loosened the strings on her purse... or rather, cut them right off.

"Okay, that's enough to buy *something*."

She'd hunted enough monsters and wasn't about to let that gold burn a hole in her pocket. She made a beeline to a shop just past the gate with the kanji for seven.

"I love how there's no risk of anyone else buying the last one..."

Finding the exact same thing you've already purchased still for sale was certainly a classic gaming experience.

On this visit, she decided to pick up a pricey mug she'd yet to acquire...and immediately found herself can't-even-buy-a-potion broke yet again.

"You're a very loyal customer! Thank you."

"Mm? Oh, uh, sure."

These were the first words the shop's owner had uttered that weren't directly related to processing a purchase, and Kasumi was rather caught off guard.

"As a token of my appreciation...please take this."

He handed her an ancient-looking piece of paper.

"A map to where my warehouse once stood. I'm too old to reach it these days. Do whatever you'd like with the contents. They'd prefer that to never-ending slumber, I'm sure."

Kasumi thanked him and left the shop, staring at the map.

"It's way out at the edge of the field... Worth a look, I guess."

She'd already bought everything in town she had her eye on.

Plus, she was so broke that the usual penalty for dying (losing half your gold) was not really a concern.

But more than anything, the potential to get something special drove her on.

Because of the perpetual night on this stratum, the field was naturally always dark. Kasumi headed for the far edge at a run, occasionally checking the map.

"Around here...no, it's a little farther this way. There!"

Her foot had struck a handle resting on the ground, just barely peeking out of the dirt.

Without a map to guide her, she never could have found it in this darkness.

She brushed the dirt off the door and pulled it open.

Dust flew everywhere, and beneath the hatch was a staircase plunging into darkness.

"...Here goes nothing."

She'd bought several lanterns since reaching this stratum, so she took one out of her inventory and headed down.

Her path was lit by nothing but the lantern's flickering red light. The only sound here came from her own footsteps.

At the bottom of the stairs, she found a steel door.

"...Promising!"

With a mix of anticipation and anxiety, Kasumi pushed it open and stepped through, raising her lantern high.

"Nothing...?"

The chamber inside was quite large...and entirely empty. The lantern light caught nothing but bare floor. There was only absolute silence and the smell of dust. She raised the lantern, bringing the corners into view, but all she found was more dirt. Not exactly what came to mind when she thought of the word *warehouse*.

"Is there some other trigger? It's not very clear what that could be..."

She couldn't just give up, though.

"Wait…" Her ears caught the sound of something breaking. "*Is there something here?*"

Her guard now up, Kasumi drew her katana and moved deeper into the room.

The lantern light revealed what had been too dark to see before.

Littered all around were the remains of the wares housed here.

Broken swords, smashed vases, shattered crystals…

And at the center of this devastation—a sword, floating in the air, wreathed in a faint purple light.

Each time it came into contact with something, sounds of destruction rang out, almost as if the blade itself was consuming whatever it touched.

"…And I'm next?!"

The floating katana seemed to notice Kasumi. Its tip turned toward her—and she readied hers.

Perhaps it viewed her as a threat—the purple glow grew brighter, coiling around the blade like smoke.

For a moment, it shivered. Then purple fire engulfed the floor and ceiling, flooding the room with light.

Kasumi took a few steps back, putting her lantern aside. The katana made no move.

"Not attacking first? No—can't let my guard down yet."

The living weapon had a sense of foreboding about it.

Her instincts were right.

A moment later, the katana shot toward her.

She exhaled, and her blade clashed against it—but the flying katana was able to move as it pleased, and it was hard to predict what direction its attack would come from.

"Fighting Shin…had unexpected benefits…! Ha…!"

She'd recently fought one of Flame Empire's top players and his flying blades in the last event.

Swatting aside this sentient katana felt awfully familiar thanks to that experience.

The loud *clang* still hanging in the air, Kasumi leaped back, waiting for her strange opponent to make its next move.

But despite keeping her watchful gaze from wavering—the sword vanished.

"Wha...?! Ah!"

The next thing she saw was a purple katana buried in her chest. And not *just* her chest.

There were more protruding from her legs, belly, arms—everywhere.

She'd seen this before—after all, it was a skill she had used herself.

When her eyes opened again, she was in the square right by the entrance to the fourth-stratum town. This was where players spawned after dying on this stratum.

"......Heh. Heh-heh-heh-heh. Fascinating... I'm gonna get my hands on that before anyone else does! No way I'm letting a *sword* beat me!"

The frustration proved to be incredibly motivating for Kasumi, who began working on a plan.

◆□◆□◆□◆□◆

A few days later, Kasumi stood before the flying katana once again.

She'd made more than *fifty* runs.

"...Okay, *this* time—!"

As she reached the base of the stairs, the blade came to meet her.

"............"

Kasumi drew her sword, visualizing her plan of attack. The blades slammed into each other.

The shrill sound of metal on metal filled the warehouse.

There was an HP bar floating over the enemy katana, and Kasumi kept a close eye on it as she fought.

"Leap!"

After she chipped a bit of the sword's health off, she bounded forward.

A moment later, multiple blades skewered the place she'd just been standing.

This katana would take certain actions at specific HP thresholds. But there were several variations, and it was extremely difficult to grasp them all. On top of that, the raw DPS of these moves could easily tear through Kasumi like tissue paper—which explained her high death count. Still, after dozens of runs, she'd learned to avoid *this* attack easily enough.

"First Blade: Heat Haze!"

Closing the gap once more, she swung her sword, then took a single step to the right.

She'd known a blade would come shooting out of the floor.

Trading blows with the floating katana, she moved a step at a time, tracing a circle around it.

More blades shot upward a beat after each step.

A moment's pause would be fatal, but she couldn't move too fast—as long as she kept circle strafing at this range, her opponent's attack pattern would remain unchanged. And there lay the key to her victory.

It had taken her a *long* time to discover this strategy.

*   *   *

As she completed a full circle, the katana's HP reached the next threshold—causing it to shift to a new phase.

The blades from the floor were replaced with purple fire raining down from above.

Coming into contact with these flames would leave her stuck at AGI 0 for ten full seconds.

The katana itself began swooping around wildly—without high Agility, these movements were impossible to evade.

Kasumi had been thwarted by this rain of fire longer than anything else.

She simply could not dodge the flames long enough to reach the next phase.

She'd been forced to go through every skill she had, looking for a way out.

"Final Blade: Misty Moon."

The results had boiled down to *get it before I get got.*

A lightning-fast twelve-hit combo struck the floating katana as if trying to snap it in half.

The sword's HP dropped like a rock, but Kasumi wasn't celebrating.

This combo would blow right through three of the katana's phases, bringing it to the final stage.

Only a few dots remained on its HP bar—but that was unavoidable.

No matter how strong her attack, no matter what tactics she used—it would *always* retain those last few points.

Kasumi's Katana Arts skill gave her a whole series of numbered moves she could call upon. Misty Moon was the greatest of these, but any uses would temporarily halve her stats—and lock the whole move set.

She had to finish this battle in that condition.

This incredible challenge was what had pushed her attempt count into the fifties.

"............"

The katana teleported to the far corner of the room, glowing with an even more ominous light.

A burst of flames encircled Kasumi, reaching as high as the ceiling before giving way to full-blown walls of fire, leaving only a path that led right to the katana.

Twenty-five yards away. The path itself was only three yards wide.

Kasumi would have to dart down this gauntlet to land her final blow.

"Hah!"

Exhaling sharply, she broke into a run—noticeably slower than before.

Not only was the katana launching blades at her, but jets of flame were shooting out of the walls on either side.

If she paused for even a second, a blade would skewer her from below.

This was the longest twenty-five yards of her life.

"Haaah!"

Batting aside a missile with the flat of her blade, she shifted her path ever so slightly, never breaking stride.

The flames would crater her AGI, so she couldn't afford to be hit by them. The blades rearing up from below were similarly fatal. But the swords flying at her from the front were another matter.

If she got this far without taking damage, she could afford to get hit by *three* of them.

*　　*　　*

She reached the halfway point in good shape, and her instinct told her it was time.

"Superspeed!"

She'd kept this in reserve to propel her through the so-far-insurmountable last stretch.

Yesterday, she'd taken a break from fighting this sword to ask Sally and Shin for help improving her ability to dodge flying blades.

The training had paid off, and she could *see* the projectiles better than ever before.

But as she got close, the attacks came too fast for her to react in time.

"C'mon...!"

She took hits to her left shoulder, her right side, and her left thigh.

Painful red sparks sprayed like fresh blood.

But *still*, Kasumi did not stop, forging ahead like a warrior possessed.

She thrust forward with the sword in her right hand—and touched the flying katana.

Instantly, the weapon lost its light and began to fall. A scabbard, completely covered in talismans, rose to catch it.

The raging walls of fire and the blades piercing her body all vanished, leaving only darkness.

"............"

Kasumi reached out and picked up the fallen katana.

"Heh-heh...ha-ha-ha! I did it! I finally did it!"

Unable to restrain her joy, she shouted in celebration as she inspected her new equipment.

Yukari, the All-Consuming Blight

[STR+30]

[Blighted Blade]

[Self-Repairing]

Blighted Blade

While equipped, provides a set of five skills, each of which comes with a cost: HP reduction, MP reduction, temporary stat reduction, permanent stat reduction, or a physical limitation.

Self-Repairing

While sheathed, regenerates durability.

"Worth a try. Let's find a monster to use this on!"

Kasumi equipped her new cursed blade and went looking for a damage sponge monster to try it on.

It didn't take her long.

"Good, good, these have loads of endurance."

As Kasumi drew her new sword, she found herself enveloped in purple smoke.

"Uhhh…hmm?"

The smoke itself was soon carried away by the wind, but it had left its mark.

Kasumi's outfit had changed dramatically.

Deep purple hakama cloaked her from the waist down while her chest and arms were wrapped in pale purple strips of cloth—and nothing else.

Purple smoke trailed from the blade and the sarashi around her arms, billowing ceaselessly behind her.

"............"

Kasumi tried to sheathe the blade but was so rattled that she missed the first time and had to take a breath before trying again.

When she did, the smoke enveloped her once more, and her clothes thankfully went back to normal.

"W-will I *ever* get used to that? I mean...*just* sarashi?"

But she couldn't bring herself to *not* use a sword this good.

She cleared her throat and drew the blade again, trying not to blush.

Four of the skill penalties were more or less self-explanatory, but *physical limitation* was somewhat mysterious, so she gave the skill a shot.

"Purple Phantom Blade!"

The skill propelled her toward the monster.

Her right hand swung.

Letting the skill take over, she let go of the blade—and then it vanished, reappearing in her left hand.

Striking home with her left, she let it go again—and once more, the blade appeared in her right hand.

Alternating hands, she charged in, driving the beast back and landing ten strikes in all.

After the final blow, she released the sword one last time and struck her palms together.

Ten blades appeared, surrounding the monster and spearing it from all sides.

A twenty-hit combo. No ordinary monster was tough enough to withstand that.

The skill ended, and the blade returned to her right hand.

"So, so good..."

Were it not for the mandatory clothing, it would be perfect—but even as that thought crossed her mind, purple smoke enveloped Kasumi once more.

"...Oh, it's gone. Wow, did I just drop the sword?"

She tried to pick it up...and belatedly realized her hand was *very small*.

"Uh..."

The system was keeping her hakama in place, but they were definitely very baggy now—and the sarashi was no longer wound tight.

At the moment, Kasumi was just under four feet tall.

"You have got to be..."

She was still gaping when another monster came running toward her.

How inconsiderate.

"Hold on...! W-wait, see how cute I am? That means you should...let me go! Argh!"

Her pleas for mercy went unheard, and she was promptly sent back to town.

When she respawned, Kasumi's sarashi had been tightened up again, but she was still tiny.

She checked her status screen.

"I'm stuck like this for *ten minutes*..."

She pulled up the hems of her hakama and waddled over to a bench, then closed her eyes, trying her best to ignore the stares of everyone standing in the square.

Katana now in hand, Kasumi turned her attention back to raising her access rank.

Elsewhere, Maple had been similarly busy. After a week of trying her best, she was lying flat out on the table at the Guild Home.

"Sallyyyy…my access rank is going nowherrrre…"

"Yeah, I'm not surprised it's rough for you," Sally said. She was sitting on the other side of the table.

The access permit quests all consisted of errands that involved running across town or venturing outside of it.

That included plenty of gathering or hunting tasks.

Kasumi had been burning through them like crazy, but for virtually everyone else, they'd been major time sinks.

Maple had sacrificed a great many things for her single-minded dedication to defense, leaving her solidly in the lowest rung for movement speed.

Sally's access was already at seven, while Maple was still at her original five.

"I wanna go further iiin!"

But even as Maple wailed, a tremor shook the entire stratum.

"Wh-what was that…?"

"I dunno…oh."

Both of them received a message from the admins.

They pulled it up and read the contents.

A player has passed torii gate nine, restoring the town to its rightful form. Additional items and quests are now available.

"Sally! Let's go right now!"

"Mm, probably worth checking out."

One step out of the Guild Home and they immediately spotted a major difference.

"Gosh…those are…"

"Yeah, clearly. Ogres…"

They were obviously not human—and it wasn't just ogres, but all manner of spirits and yokai. All of them were walking around like they owned the place. They were selling arcane potions and items decorated with esoteric writing.

The fourth stratum had become a town of yokai and witchcraft.

"Sally, are you gonna freak out on me?"

Maple was pointing at a wobbling wisp, the exact sort of thing that usually frightened her friend.

"It's not coming at me or trying to scare me... As long as it leaves me alone..."

Clearly, she wasn't ever gonna be a fan.

One eye firmly on the wisp, Sally asked, "Think it was Kasumi?"

"She *was* really going at it."

They considered her the most likely suspect...

...and they were right on the money.

Kasumi was sitting just inside the gate with the kanji for nine.

The moment she'd stepped through, purple smoke had come pouring out of the buildings around her, accompanied by chanting and blinding lights. Yokai after yokai had rushed past her, and she'd been so shocked that she lost her footing.

Only when the admin message arrived did she recover her bearings.

"That would explain it. Okay. Whew..."

She got back up and glanced around the new district.

"The next gate is pretty close."

A single road led between them.

She weaved through the throngs of yokai and passed the shops lining both sides. At the end, she found herself at the tower they'd seen looming overhead this whole time.

Before that stood a final gate, with the kanji for ten.

And by that gate was a sign.

THE NEXT RULER SHALL BE WHOEVER FINDS THE RED OGRE'S HORN, THE DRAGON'S SORE SCALE, AND THE DIVINE DEW.

After reading that, Kasumi ran through everything she'd bought so far.

"They definitely weren't available in any stores...but there's more items now, so I guess I'll have to make the rounds again."

Gathering information on these three items was the perfect excuse. Excited to see what new treasures she might discover, Kasumi resumed her grand shopping tour.

Nearly every player was doing the same—seeing what new things might await after the town's transformation. Between the excited players and the new yokai NPCs, the peaceful town was a hive of activity.

Maple and Sally were in a nearby shop, checking if there was anything new on offer.

The shop's owner had once been human, but now she had a fox's tail and ears.

"She was in disguise?"

"Seems like it."

It was time to examine the new merchandise.

There was so much. Some practical, some not.

"Look, Maple!" Sally said, holding up two sets of three paper charms bound with string.

The set in her left hand was white, and the one in her right was black.

"They do different things?"

"Yup. The black one randomly disables one of your opponent's skills for three minutes. The white one lets you pick a skill in advance and takes the hit if someone tries to seal it."

And since there were three of each, you could use them that many times.

"Interesting..."

"You can only have one set of each color, though."

"...Worth buying?"

"I think so. Might come in handy someday."

Certainly couldn't hurt to have on hand. Each of them bought one set of each color.

"Sally, Sally, look what I found!"

Maple was holding up fake horns and ears.

"Wanna try 'em on?" Sally said. The signs in the store clearly said this was allowed.

"Mm...I'll go with this one!"

Maple had picked out some very curly horns.

"Hmm...," Sally said.

"I thought these would look good when I'm all woolly."

"Oh, right, your sheep form. Fair! I think they would."

"Then this one's for you, Sally."

"Uh, no, I'm not..."

Despite her hesitance, Maple handed her a set of white fox ears and a matching tail.

"Just like Oboro!"

"I guess... Well, maybe I can try it when nobody else is around... I don't think I'm brave enough for the tail, though."

If these took off and everyone else started wearing them, she'd reconsider it then. Sally and Maple both made their purchases and went outside.

"I've got some errands to run, so I'd better log out..."

"Sure thing! Bye, Sally."

"See you later, Maple."

Sally vanished in a puff of light.

On her own, Maple pondered her next move—then she saw a familiar face passing.

"Oh, Mii! She's headed…what *is* that way?"

Mii had taken several furtive looks around before slipping down a narrow alley, so naturally, Maple followed her.

They'd met during the last event and become friends after, so she figured she should say hi.

After several turns, she heard Mii's voice up ahead.

There was no real reason to hide, but Maple found herself lingering at the last corner, peeking around it.

"All right…just a little relaxation before I go hunt those monsters," Mii said.

She had her menu open to change her equipment.

And not just her equipment—she also used an item that changed her entire appearance.

Her red hair became long and white, and her clothes were now blue with white highlights. At a glance, no one would think it was Mii at all.

Red was her most defining feature.

"Here I come!"

Mii opened the door and stepped in.

"……Was that something I wasn't supposed to see? Agh!"

Maple hadn't meant to sneak around and spy on her.

She decided not to tell anyone but figured it was best to give Mii a heads up.

"Uh, this shop is…"

She checked the little sign outside. It said… THE FLOATING CUDDLE ROOM.

"…Okay! Here goes."

Maple opened the door and stepped inside. She paid the girl working the counter and went on through.

The room she entered was filled with fluffy cats, all suspended in midair.

Mii was in the middle, a look of rapture on her face.

When she spotted Maple, she quickly hid behind a cat.

Despite her disguise, she knew she'd be recognized up close.

After all…her *face* hadn't changed.

Maple went over and fessed up, apologizing for the inadvertent discovery.

"Oh, don't worry. Maybe I wanted someone to know. Keeping up the act is getting exhausting…ah-ha-ha…"

"I really didn't mean to! If there's anything I can do for you, just let me know!"

"…Well, if you help me hunt some monsters later…?"

Maple was more than happy to oblige. But first, she joined Mii and enjoyed the pile of fluff.

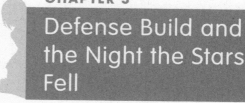

CHAPTER 3

Defense Build and the Night the Stars Fell

Mii changed back to her usual red clothes and partied up with Maple, and then they headed out of town together. She was back in character.

"So, uh, why *do* you role-play?" Maple asked.

"I just…missed my chance to stop," Mii admitted.

"…Then let's call it our secret!"

"Um…heh-heh. Thanks."

Mii looked relieved, and Maple gave her a reassuring smile for good measure. Together, they set out to find some monsters.

"I'm really slow, so… Atrocity! I'll give you a ride wherever you want to go."

"…C-climbing aboard!"

Mii clambered up a hideous leg, taking a seat on Maple's back. She had not imagined herself doing *this* today.

But as soon as she suggested a destination, Maple said, "You got it! Away we go!"

The Maple monster lurched into motion, looking far more terrifying than any of the actual monsters around.

*　　*　　*

She ran for a while, and they reached their destination. It was an abandoned village filled with run-down houses—all of which had paper talismans plastered on them.

Mii leaped down, stretched, and activated a skill.

"Here goes nothing... Flame Empress!"

As if in answer, wisp after wisp appeared in the air around them. These tried to attack with fires of their own, but Mii's inferno struck first. However, fire-based monsters weathered burning attacks well, and she was taking her share of hits back. Knowing this was bound to happen, Mii had been ready to do some fancy footwork to minimize incoming damage, but before she did, Maple activated *her* skill.

"Martyr's Devotion!"

This skill completely protected Mii from all attacks.

Terrifying to fight against, but when Maple was on your side, you might as well forget evading and blocking even existed.

Mii no longer needed to take any defensive measures.

With Maple beside her, she could focus entirely on carving through monster HP.

They wandered, hunting as they went, and once there was nothing left to go after, Mii went limp.

"...No wonder we couldn't win," she muttered.

She sat down by the shore of a lake. They'd started in the early evening, and it was now so late the date was about to change.

"Thanks, Maple. Sorry if I've kept you up."

Mii usually had to stay very focused when she hunted, so being able to relax and chat had been too much fun to stop. She had even unconsciously slipped into her normal speaking voice.

"Nah, I had fun, too! But maybe we should wrap things up. I *am* getting sleepy."

It was late in the real world, too. Maple was usually logged out by now.

"Thanks again! I'll call it, too. I don't usually get to go all out like that, so I'm extra wiped."

"Oh, that reminds me! How about one for the road?"

Maple released her Atrocity form, falling out of the monster's belly with a *splat*.

Once she was human again, she activated a different skill, turning into a two-yard-tall ball of fluff.

"Come on in!"

"Uh, inside that...? S-sure..."

Gingerly, Mii parted the wool.

Once inside, she found herself cushioned from every angle, and all her tension just started to melt away.

"Oh...this *is* nice."

"Glad to hear it."

Mii burrowed in above Maple and spent several minutes like that.

But right as they hit peak relaxation, they felt something tugging on the wool.

"Wh-what's that?"

"Hmm?"

Both their faces popped out of the woolly ball's side.

The fluffball had been freed from the constraints of gravity and was bobbing along just above the lake.

"Maple, wh-what's going on?"

"Don't ask me!"

They reached the center of the lake and began to ascend.

"Is this…some sort of Easter egg?"

"Maybe? If we fall, I'll keep us both safe!"

But once they were a good twenty yards above the lake's surface, the water itself began rising upward as well until a column of it enveloped them.

That only lasted a second—an instant later, they were bathed in light and found themselves *somewhere else.*

"W-we'd better get out."

Mii squirmed her way out of the wool, landing to one side.

Maple was helpless to free herself, so she asked Mii to burn the wool off.

She felt her feet hit the ground, except technically, it was something else.

"Where…are we?"

"I think…these are clouds?"

The earth they were expecting had been replaced with soft white…clouds.

Maple looked up, checking the skies above.

"So many stars…!"

She'd never seen them shine so bright. She couldn't tear her eyes away.

"Yeah, it's gorgeous. The kind of night you expect the stars to fall."

For a while, they gazed in rapture with nary a word passing between them.

The sight was so breathtaking that it stripped away the drowsiness Maple had been feeling, and eventually, it occurred to her to look around.

"…What now? Keep going? I mean, we've got no idea how to come back here even if we want to later…"

Mii agreed with this suggestion, and they clambered over a low cloud wall, moving onward.

Before long, they found a cloud road leading straight ahead. It stretched away into the distance, and there was every indication that something was waiting for them at the end.

It was just wide enough for them to walk side-by-side.

"Mm? Maple! Look up!"

"Up? Martyr's Devotion!"

Maple quickly activated her skill again, keeping Mii safe.

She was just in time, too—because a moment later, glowing objects began falling on them.

Maple took several hits as she backed away.

And that made the shower stop.

Looking closer, it was clear what these things were.

"You were right, Mii! The stars *did* fall."

"I didn't mean it *literally*..."

"Hard to tell how fast they were going, but I can soak them. Let's keep moving."

They set out once more.

The stars began falling on them again, but they didn't do anything besides bounce off Maple.

"Sally could probably dodge 'em all."

"I dunno, there's a *lot*."

They were getting pelted relentlessly.

It didn't seem like something you could just slip through.

They forged on, and after a short while, the end of their path came into view.

"A seriously big one is coming right at us..."

The words had barely left Maple's mouth as a massive star scored a bull's-eye on her. Mii flinched, but Maple didn't even break her stride.

"No problemo! And here we are!"

At the end of the road was a wall made of clouds, with a tunnel in it.

Having come this far, they *had* to go in. They proceeded with caution.

The tunnel wasn't particularly long, and they soon came out the other side.

Light poured down from above.

Softly, like unspooling thread.

These rays led to a vessel made from clouds.

"Oh…"

"Wow…"

They drew closer and touched the light within.

It didn't *feel* like anything, but both of them received an item.

"Divine Dew?"

"Doesn't say what you use it for… Maybe it's a crafting material?"

"Is this all we get here? What do you think, Mii?"

"Probably. It was a straight path, after all."

Maple nodded in agreement, and they decided to end their search.

"Okay, this time we're wrapping up for real! This was fun. Let me know if you wanna play together again!"

"Definitely. I'd love to. I've had enough for one day, though. Thanks again."

And with their unexpected adventure over, they both logged out.

The next day…

Maple told Sally about her impromptu team-up with Mii and about the Divine Dew.

"Hmm…it might be some sort of key item, so better hold on to it," Sally said. "But you and Mii wound up exploring together, huh?"

"Yeah, uh…one thing led to another."

It was pretty normal for Maple to just do things her way, accidentally stumbling into greatness, and Sally had always figured as long as she was having fun, nothing could be better. As such, she asked no more. Since Maple had promised Mii to keep her secret, she didn't volunteer anything else and changed topics.

"I've really gotta get my access rank up."

This stratum had far more things to do than any before, and every day felt like a whole new event.

"Reaching ten soon would be nice. After that, I'll just be waiting for you at the finish line."

"I *will* catch up!"

Kasumi had been first, but one by one, other players were getting to the ninth checkpoint.

And eventually, one of them spread the word. By early November, everyone knew the town's ultimate goal—

To gather three key items.

The leaders of Flame Empire and Maple Tree had already claimed one—the Divine Dew. They'd spread the word through their respective guilds, and everyone had tried to get a hold of it, but the members of Flame Empire were struggling with the sheer DPS of the stars that rained on that cloudy dungeon.

Mii wound up regularly calling Maple in to help get them through.

The payments for these escort missions kept her wallet in good health.

Meanwhile, the members of Maple Tree had taken a single run all together, and then Sally took a solo run afterward, easily scoring enough Divine Dew for everyone in their guild. As long as Maple was around, it was nothing more than a pleasant stroll.

The only question that remained was where to find the other items.

◆□◆□◆□◆□◆

A few days later, the player base's combined efforts finally revealed how to get the other two key items.

The info began to circulate, and it wasn't long before anyone could easily obtain detailed intel on the monsters protecting them.

There was no requirement to solo the monsters, but they were tough, and not many players had managed to beat them.

"Hmm... I'll pass for now, then. We'll go once everyone's ready."

Sally had concluded that it would be a bit rough on her own.

And she had plenty of powerful allies to rely on.

"Focusing on my access rank seems better."

Right as she hopped up to leave, the door opened.

It was a familiar face.

"About to head out?"

A mage from the Order of the Holy Sword—Frederica.

She'd developed a habit of popping in, challenging Sally to a duel, losing, and dragging herself home.

Sally may have won every time, but Frederica's attacks were getting very close to actually connecting.

"Yeah, gotta waste some trash mobs to boost my access rank."

"Gotcha... Well, I don't wanna stand around waiting, so I'll help out. Let's get that out of the way and then duke it out!"

"Works for me. C'mon, time to grind."

"I've got a whole new plan for taking ya on!"

"You always say that."

"What choice do I have when you always ruin my latest plans on first contact?! Just let me land one hit!"

Frederica was perfectly aware that Sally didn't have the endurance to survive that hit. And Frederica's build was all about AOE attacks.

Sally couldn't afford to make a single mistake.

Wondering how she could win this time, she and Frederica headed out into the field.

"Magic *is* pretty nice."

While Sally had to cut down each target individually, Frederica could just bombard whole swaths at once.

Seeing her in action made Sally want more magic.

The only spells she was using at the moment were defensive ones—anything that turned attacks away from her.

Her MP wasn't *too* shabby, but she'd put most of her focus on AGI and STR, her primary damage drivers.

She'd focused on leveling more than Maple and was closing the gap.

Sally was currently level 34.

"And that's the last one!"

Sally dealt the finishing blow, and the monster's HP bar disintegrated.

As it did, Sally's level went up to 35. With this, she met another requirement to raise her access rank.

"Mm…mm! Hee-hee."

"What's so funny?"

"Oh, just got a level-up at the same time. I'm all done here. Wanna have that duel now?"

Frederica nodded emphatically—clearly, she hadn't forgotten why she'd come in the first place.

Once both of them agreed to the duel, a bright light enveloped them. The sensation of the teleportation was very familiar by now. Once more, they were in a zone cut off from the rest of the world.

The countdown began, and the pre-fight tension took hold.

As the duel started in earnest, Sally took a step toward Frederica...

"Oh?"

...and then drew up short.

If Frederica had commenced with her usual barrage, Sally would've had no trouble handling it, but this time around, she'd opened their match by making a bunch of walls—impeding Sally's movement.

Water and sand were closing in on her from all sides.

"Leap!"

There wasn't an attack she needed to avoid or anything, but Sally took off diagonally, moving forward while angling left.

She just had a bad feeling. A sense of impending danger.

Sally had honed this instinct during the last event, and she let it guide her.

She quickly slipped past the walls, so when wind blades tore through them a moment later, they caught nothing.

Sally had kept her defense and HP at rock bottom, so a broadside like this would instantly take her out if *any* of it hit.

"Precognition again?!"

"Nothing that fancy!"

Sally was already charging Frederica at top speed, forcing her to quickly switch to plan B.

""Ah!""

It was pure chance.

Their yelps of surprise came at the same instant only because of a fluke in timing.

Frederica had thrown up more walls, and one had just happened to catch Sally's toes ever so slightly, making her suddenly stumble.

She lost her balance—but that actually brought her outside the path of the wind blades.

"Multi-Firebolt!" Frederica yelled, not about to let this chance slip past. This was the spell she used the most, and she was casting it before her mind had even fully processed what was happening.

Sally had no choice but to keep rolling to avoid it.

To Frederica, the next bit happened in slow motion.

The last firebolt landed square on Sally's shoulder and burst.

That meant she was physically there—not a mirage.

Frederica was sure she'd finally won.

"Yesss!"

Pumping her fist, she shivered with delight.

But the victory she'd yearned for made her careless.

She didn't notice Sally's approach. By the time she realized Sally was still alive, there was a dagger buried deep in her chest.

"What the…?"

"Afraid you were counting some unhatched chickens there."

Before she could fire back, Frederica's HP was gone.

The last thing she saw before being transported back was Sally's HP bar—still *completely* full.

"Um…huh? How?!"

"I can't tell you all my secrets. We're enemies."

"Urgh, that's true. Mm. Fine! I'll win next time! You'll see."

She waved good-bye and ran off.

"...That was seriously close," Sally muttered. "I really can't let my guard down."

She glanced at her status.

Shed Skin

Negate a fatal blow once a day.
50% boost to AGI for one minute.

A skill she'd acquired for reaching level 35 without taking damage.

And because she'd acquired this, she hadn't been *quite* as focused.

Knowing she couldn't *ever* afford to take a hit had helped her concentrate.

"Gotta do more evasion practice. Hmm... I can't afford to get damaged for the first time until the big day."

Muttering to herself, she ran off to bait some trash mobs into chasing after her.

CHAPTER 4

Defense Build and the Dragon Hunt

While Sally was retraining her dodges, Maple was doing access permit quests.

There was a lot to do on this stratum, meaning the town and field were equally teeming with players.

The Maple Tree members were every bit as busy, and their top players were always on the go, everyone pursuing their own personal agendas.

The "big day" came a few days after Sally hit level 35.

The guild had decided to go slay a dragon together.

They finally found a day when everyone could participate and took advantage of it.

And with Maple in the party, there was almost no chance of them wiping.

Sally's info had helped them figure out a plan that would take advantage of everyone's skills, allowing them to beat this thing and claim the Dragon's Sore Scales.

*　　*　　*

"The intel says it flies around, spitting balls of electricity. When it gets low, you hit it with spells and arrows. But it's got decent magic resistance, meaning bows tend to do the heavy lifting. Drop the HP far enough and it'll start skimming the ground, charging, claw slashes, breath attacks. Only the claws are piercing. Then it'll back away after a bit by flying. The fight won't be in a dungeon. That's about all I got."

"So we've got this in the bag," Chrome said. There was a direct correlation between their odds of winning and the number of attacks that worked on Maple.

"I also picked up Dragon Slayer on this floor," Kasumi said. "I'll hit it with that when it's close to the ground."

As the name suggested, her skill increased damage against dragon-type monsters.

"Yui and I'll do the same."

The twins were on the ground squad, and this team composition meant the dragon would likely not survive to fly again after coming down the first time.

If it couldn't break through Maple and Chrome to take out the twins, death was virtually inevitable.

"Then Maple and I will hit it in the air? We're the ones with distance attacks."

"That's right, Kanade. I think that's the only way."

Even if it did resist a lot of magic damage, Kanade's spells would still definitely help.

"It might take a while...but we're taking that thing down."

Sally got up to go, but Maple raised her hand.

"Um, I have an idea," she offered.

"Lay it on us."

Maple began to explain her cunning scheme.

◆□◆□◆□◆□◆

Maple Tree was climbing a mountain, bound for the peak with the magic circle that would whisk them to the dragon fight.

Any monsters that swooped at the party bounced off Maple's defense, and the other seven made short work of them.

"Here we are!"

"Yep, that's the one."

The glowing circle was waiting for them.

Once they stepped in, they'd be in the combat zone.

"Right, just do what Maple said!"

And with that, everyone jumped on and vanished in a puff of light.

The battlefield looked a lot like the wasteland where Maple had fought the demon.

The sky above was dark and ominous, and the white scales of the dragon were clearly visible against it.

It was too high up for even spells to reach. And from that elevation, it was flinging crackling white balls down at them.

Its aim proved true, but Maple took no damage, so everything was hunky-dory.

"Yup, we're good."

"Cool. Maple, do your thang."

"Sounds good! Kasumi?"

"Ready."

Paying no heed to the monster's attacks, they got ready to fight.

Maple deployed her Machine God kit, fully prepared to take flight. Kasumi found a way to fit between the artillery pieces to cling on to Maple's back and used an Iz-made Doping Seed to boost her STR.

Maple glanced up, pinpointing the dragon's location, and then aimed her barrels at the ground.

"Here we go!"

Flames and explosions scorched the earth as the two girls rocketed skyward.

They went *through* a lightning ball and kept hurtling toward the dragon's maw.

As they drew near, Kasumi leaped down onto the dragon's head, and Maple flew alongside it. Both activated their skills.

"Saturating Chaos! Hydra!"

"Final Blade: Misty Moon! Purple Phantom Blade!"

Maple's attacks shot through the flying dragon, and Kasumi raced down its back as her attacks activated, each hit knocking off chunks of its HP.

A monster designed to be whittled away with ranged spells was easily dropped to the first HP threshold.

Maple reached the tail first, summoned Syrup, and ordered it to hover. Then she used the recoil from her attacks to land on its back.

"Maple! Leap!"

Shrouded in purple smoke and tiny after using her ability, Kasumi more or less tumbled her way toward Maple, who caught her, eyes wide.

Kasumi still wasn't used to this form and had lost her sword again—it was falling toward the ground as the dragon descended.

"*Sigh...* We might not have needed Purple Phantom Blade."

"Wow! I've never seen anything like this. Look at you!"

Maple was beaming at her, and the close examination made Kasumi squirm.

"Don't stare… It's a whole thing, I know…"

"Oh, sorry. Let's watch the others take their turn!"

"It would be a good skill if it weren't for this…"

Chrome saw the dragon headed their way and lowered his shield. (He'd been tanking the lightning balls in Maple's absence.)

"Incoming!"

"We're ready for it!"

Mai and Yui had their hammers raised, standing on either side of the dragon's aggressive flight path.

They'd used Doping Seeds while Kanade cast all the STR buff support spells he could muster, and Sally had even busted out her Inspire skill for practically the first time. Their effective STR was as high as it could possibly be.

Roaring, the dragon swooped toward them.

Its attack pattern set in stone, the ferocious creature was forced to charge blindly into certain death.

""Farshot!""

Their hurled hammers released four shock waves, each striking the dragon head-on. It had 80 percent of its health remaining, and these hits instantly took that down to 0.

"Everyone talks about Maple, but these two are plenty nuts in their own right…"

"Yuuup."

"Did I stack *too much* support magic? Oh, here come Maple and Kasumi."

After soundly defeating the boss in less than a minute, they now had enough Dragon's Sore Scales for every guild member.

Nobody else could match their clear speed, and for most of the player base, the dragon remained a very tough boss.

*　　*　　*

On Syrup's back, Kasumi got her clothes back in order, then went to collect her katana. When that was done, Maple Tree took the circle back to the original mountain, and their hunt was over.

Since Kasumi was still struggling with her tiny form, everyone took a Syrup ride down the slope.

"How is it you can run in that body?" Kasumi asked, referring to Maple's monstrous Atrocity form.

"I just can!"

"...Helpful."

Kasumi looked like she had expected nothing less.

"You'll be back to normal in ten minutes?" Chrome asked. "In that case, wanna head straight into the ogre fight?"

This was the other boss—the one that dropped the final item they needed.

"I'm up for it! Let's go!"

"Why not? We've got the intel we need."

They'd shaved a *lot* of time off their original schedule, and everyone agreed they might as well use that to beat the other boss.

"The ogre's on the ground, so if we can have the twins massacre it before it has a chance to hit the second phase... You two up for it?"

""Totally!""

"I'll put Martyr's Devotion up, just in case."

And so they entered the ogre's lair.

The ogre *looked* fearsome, but ten seconds later...it was gone in a puff of light.

With all three items in hand, Kasumi split off from the party and hurried to the tenth torii gate. The rest of the team had yet to raise their access ranks enough, so she was going solo.

"Whew... Well, let's see what's waiting behind door number ten."

Kasumi became the first person to step through the gate into the tower.

"Guess I start climbing."

The passageway and stairs inside were lit by purple fires. There were no visible side rooms to speak of.

Staying on guard, she headed for the top.

"Here we are... Seems like the coast is clear."

At the top of the stairs, she found a pair of closed sliding doors.

Surely, there must be *something* behind them.

Kasumi took a deep breath and slid them open.

The only remarkable thing about the room beyond was the tatami floors.

At the very back of it sat a two-horned ayakashi clad in hakama and a kimono as white as his hair.

His features resembled those of the ogre, but he was far more human-looking than the four-yard-tall muscle-bound monster they'd annihilated earlier that day.

The sign outside the building had mentioned "the next ruler." Kasumi assumed this was the *current* ruler. She waited to see what he would do.

"Oh...? I did not expect a *human*," he said, rising to his feet.

He strode toward her. At least two yards tall, he definitely cut an imposing figure.

"You have the items? Then come this way."

When he was sure Kasumi had all three key items, he turned

his back on her, heading back the way he'd come. A magic circle appeared on the floor, and he vanished into it.

"Why not?"

Steeling herself, Kasumi stepped onto the circle. She then found herself in another wasteland, much like the stage for the dragon fight. A quick scan of the area didn't turn up a single boulder, much less a tree.

The ruler was not far away.

"I was not expecting your kind," he said. "Allow me to test if your human body has the strength for the task."

"............."

"Defeat me! Accomplish this and the throne is yours."

Kasumi had seen this coming and calmly drew her katana.

"Shall we begin, human?"

No sooner had the words reached her ears than white light poured forth from his hand before coalescing into a blade.

"Challenge accepted!" Kasumi cried, more than ready. She advanced.

The ruler swung his blade down, heedless of the distance between them.

"Wha...?!"

The blade reached out, leaving a deep gouge in her.

Before she recovered from her shock, her HP hit zero, and she vanished.

Breaking her stride had proven fatal. She waited for her respawn.

Back in town, Kasumi checked to see if she still had the key items. Relief flooded her when she confirmed they were still in her possession. She had the right to challenge the ruler again.

And she was looking forward to it. "Hmm…very high damage. This is gonna take a few runs. At the very least, I'll have to learn to dodge *that*."

She'd died numerous times getting her blighted blade and had learned to recover quickly from an ignoble defeat.

◆□◆□◆□◆□◆

A week later, Kasumi was slumped against the table at the Guild Home.

"Sally? What's wrong with Kasumi?"

"She can't seem to beat the big boss. He's mad strong, apparently. I imagine it's gonna be a while before you get there… Wanna know what he's like?"

"One hundred percent!"

Maple sounded eager, so Sally gave her the full rundown.

"Solo-only one-on-one fight. The boss matches your weapon choice, so it'd be daggers for me. Most importantly, that changes how he fights. Right now, people think staves might be easiest—magic focus, all ranged attacks, etcetera…but nobody's managed to beat him yet. It's bad enough that people are starting to think there must be a trigger somewhere to weaken him."

She ran down several weapon types and what details about the boss's attack patterns had become public knowledge.

"You haven't made it there yet, right?"

"Nope. Still can't get in."

Sally's current access rank was one notch too low.

But it wouldn't be long now.

"You gonna try?"

"Hmm, I'll do battles where the odds are against me, but not when I have *no* chance. These AOE attacks are too strong."

And that meant Sally was already convinced she couldn't do it.

"If even *you* can't do it, it must be *really* strong."

"Yeah. I mean, I'd like to give it a shot someday. If we could fight it together, I'm sure we'd figure something out, but..."

That wasn't an option, period, so there was little use talking about it.

"And that's how Kasumi got like this?"

Kasumi was a shell of her former self—the fate of any player who'd been banging their head against this boss.

"Yup. Oh, there's gonna be an event soon. It'll be something like the bull hunt, apparently."

"Ugh. I'll stick to raising my access rank, then."

Some events were just not Maple's style.

With Atrocity, she could probably do better than last time, but it was already firmly lodged in her mind as *no fun*.

She made up her mind to ignore it completely and focus on her other goals.

"Good plan. There's more than enough to do as is."

"I'll be working on my access all through the event, but first...I wanna explore some more."

Maple put sheep horns on her head, changed into her kimono, and went out on the town.

"Now what? Where should I go?"

Arms folded, she started wandering aimlessly.

As she pondered, her legs carried her past an armor shop.

"Come to think of it, I haven't been in *any* of these."

Maple only ever used her unique gear or things Iz had made for her, so she'd never really wondered what stores had for sale before.

"Hellooo," she called out to announce her presence as she stepped inside one.

She looked around the interior. There was gear both beautiful and bizarre but, naturally, none of it anywhere near as good as what she had.

"I've got plenty of money, so I *could* buy something...or order a custom-made item..."

Ultimately, she did a circuit of the shop without finding anything she wanted. When she got back to the counter up front, she saw a poster on the wall behind the owner that said the purchase of five items came with a special bonus.

"In that case, I should *definitely* buy something."

She selected five cheap items and got a scroll from the seller.

"Quick Change?"

It was a skill anyone could use and everyone knew about.

But everyone in Maple Tree was too busy with their own stuff, and only Maple ever changed her gear to begin with, so word had not reached her ears.

Quick Change

Changes your gear to a preset configuration. Use again to change back.

"Nice, nice! I'd better set this up..."

A small quality-of-life improvement, but she left the shop satisfied.

◆□◆□◆□◆□◆

Maple wandered a while longer but came back to the Guild Home without anything else new.

* * *

As she came in, Mai and Yui looked up.

"Oh! Maple!" Yui cried, running over to her.

"What? Something wrong?"

"We have to fight a monster we can't beat for a quest. Can you help?"

"Please!"

They both bowed their heads in unison.

"Sure thing! I don't have anything better to do anyhow."

"Thank you! Chrome and Kanade are both out, so we didn't know who else to ask!"

The only other person home was Iz.

Primarily a crafter, she wasn't exactly the first person most people asked for help with fighting a tough enemy.

"Then let's do this! Show me where it's at!"

""Okay!""

A ten-minute Syrup ride across the field later, they reached their destination.

It looked like an old battlefield, the ground covered in broken swords and bits of armor.

"Um, the monster here is immune to physical attacks. So this is all you!"

"Uh...then I guess Hydra?"

"I *think* that should work."

Once she was briefed, Maple brought Syrup closer to the ground, activated Martyr's Devotion, and drank a potion to recover her HP. Now she was ready for combat.

"And the monster is...over there!"

She'd spotted a bundle of shredded robes paired with a rusty floating longsword.

Clearly a ghost of some kind, which explained why physical attacks didn't work.

"All righty then, Hydr... Huh? The thing vanished."

"This monster can do that...? Sorry, we had no idea."

The twins had suffered two quick defeats before they decided to go for help. Consequently, they hadn't seen the monster's full bag of tricks.

None of them were particularly well-versed in the art of scouring forums for intel, so their knowledge of this monster was quite limited.

"Now it's right on top of us!"

The apparition had approached without being seen or heard and swung its blade right at Maple, who failed to react in time.

There was a sound like something shattering as the glowing circle generated by Martyr's Devotion vanished.

"Eep? Wait— Cover!"

The monster had taken another swing, this time aimed at Yui, and Maple barely caught it in time. It had actually been a while since she'd used *this* skill.

The monster backed off and then turned invisible again.

"Martyr's Devotion! I-it won't activate?! Oh, it's sealed!"

When Maple and Sally had been exploring together, they'd bought charms that could ward off seals, but she'd used those to protect Absolute Defense, Giant Killing, and Fortress.

Not Martyr's Devotion.

"Um...then how about...Wool Up!"

Maple was suddenly a ball of fuzz, and the twins quickly figured out her plan. They dropped their weapons and burrowed in.

Maple popped her face out the front and called, "You got me?"

""We do!""

They squirmed around inside the wool until they were under

Maple, who had shifted around until she was lying facedown. Then they put their legs down, hefting the whole ball of fuzz.

Maple's face was still poking out of the front of it.

"Mai, it's on the left!"

"Okay!"

Mai and Yui rotated Maple's face to the left.

The monster took another swing at Yui.

"Incoming!"

They both crouched down, hiding inside the wool.

The monster's attack hit nothing but the fuzz over Maple's head instead.

"Hydra!"

Maple had popped one hand out of the ball, and a stream of poison shot forth from her short sword.

It was too close to miss—the monster's HP bar started going down.

It seemed like this foe wouldn't require her instant death skill.

"Whew…and it's dead! Um, how many of those do you need?"

"Ten, please!"

"Got it! Let's just stay like this, then."

A plan had formed. Mai and Yui hefted her up, made sure they had a good grip, and began hauling her around.

Then they stepped right in the lake of poison, which killed them both.

"Whoa! Uh, what happened?!"

Maple fell to the ground with a *splat*.

She called out, but neither twin answered.

"Mm? Oh…"

Maple looked down at the purple puddle that was clearly the cause.

She hastily activated Atrocity and ran back to town to pick them up.

◆□◆□◆□◆□◆

Meanwhile, Chrome and Kanade—who the twins had *meant* to call on—were out hunting monsters with Marx from Flame Empire and Drag from the Order.

"You sure are good at tanking."

Drag was the party's main DPS, while the other three backed him up.

"Yeah? I mean, that's kinda Maple's thing..."

"She doesn't count. She's...something else," Marx muttered.

In his mind, Chrome was the real great shielder.

"We talk about Maple that way ourselves, I guess."

"Maybe? I mean, she isn't *always* up to something outrageous the way she is during events. Her actual shield skills aren't that great, probably 'cause she doesn't need 'em."

Her body deflected swords, spears, arrows, and spells all on its own.

An unquenchable thirst for ever-greater defense had left her with less need for defensive *actions* than anyone else in the game.

"Pain's all fired up about beating her, but I've given up on it. I think his build is on the right track, though. Hits hard, hits fast..."

"It would still be rough," Drag admitted. He looked around. No monsters anywhere in sight.

"Time we moved on?" Marx suggested. "I think we killed everything."

He was right. The party started searching for new hunting grounds.

*　　*　　*

And on their way to the next destination…they saw the Maple monster charging by.

"So she *is* always like that."

"Maybe she is. You win this round."

The four of them stared after her as if time itself had stopped.

CHAPTER 5

Defense Build and the Fifth Event

The first week of December brought with it the fifth event, which was all about exploring the existing fields. Players got points for beating a specific monster type and competed to see who could get the most. And while it was active, the fields were covered in white as snow fell softly from the sky.

"It's gonna stay like this all month," Sally said, appreciating the view through the window of their fourth-stratum home.

"It *does* look pretty," Maple said. "And it doesn't make it harder to walk!"

"True. Welp, I'm gonna go slice and dice some event monsters."

"Have fun!"

Sally peeled her face off the window and went out the door.

Alone, Maple got up from the window seat, too.

"This time…different monsters give different points, huh?"

There were now four types of target monster.

Each of them had different spawn rates and point values. The rarer they were, the more points players would get for defeating them—and the game developers had said they had a low chance of dropping rare items, too.

"Well, if I see any of the rare ones, I'll take 'em out," Maple muttered. "The lower point monsters are too fast, so there's no point even chasing after them."

With her mind made up, she left home. Her participation in this event would be entirely secondary to raising her access rank.

Maple opened the door and stepped out into the snow.

Having snowflakes dancing in the air really changed the atmosphere, and she was enjoying just walking around in it.

Her current quest involved gathering Soul Fragments, and that had to be done on the field to the west, but she took her time, savoring the journey.

"And I'm here!"

This area was filled with abandoned houses. Maple drew her short sword, deployed her mounted guns, and then began her circuit.

She soon found some blue fireballs floating toward her. These dropped the item she was after.

"Gotcha!"

They weren't a significant threat, and her bullets were merciless—the battle was over in seconds.

"Whew…oh, nice. Today's my lucky day!"

These fireballs did *not* have a generous drop rate, and if the fight dragged on too long, they'd vanish like the monsters she'd helped the twins with.

She scooped up their drops, pleased with her good fortune, and headed out in search of more prey.

"Heh-heh-heh… What a run!"

Maple had been fighting living fireballs for half an hour, and now she only needed one last Soul Fragment to complete the quest.

The fireballs were spawning faster than she'd ever seen them, and she was thrilled.

"All right! We're doing great! Just one more!"

She was excited—but odds are ever variable.

For the next hour and a half, Maple didn't even *see* another fireball.

Right when she thought things were going well, she got incredibly unlucky.

Maple was starting to feel like she should take a break.

So she put the fireballs out of her mind and sat down against a tree, deciding to enjoy the snowy view.

"Ugh, I'm so tired... That last torii gate seems so far away..."

Once again, she had no idea how Kasumi had burned through all these quests so fast.

"There are *some* event monsters around..."

In the distance, she could see a white wolf. She took a potshot at it.

"Score! Nice...*sigh*."

One wolf wasn't going to make a difference.

"Okay, okay, let's find one last fireball and get this over with."

Maple jumped up, remotivated and ready to resume the grind.

She narrowed her eyes, scanning her surroundings, determined not to miss a single fireball.

"Finally!"

Spotting a wisp of flame out of the corner of her eye, she trained her cannons in that direction and hosed the area with bullets. This was completely overkill. Bullet after bullet struck the fireball. It never had a hope of avoiding this fate, and it quickly turned to motes of light.

"Whew...done at last."

Maple collected her drop and checked her inventory, making sure she had the necessary number of Soul Fragments.

"Good! Man, that took forever. And I thought I was having a good day, too..."

Her progress had only been good in the beginning.

She stretched and then turned to leave. It was time to turn this quest in.

But once again, the odds do ebb and flow.

"Mm?"

There was a *scrunch* behind her. She turned to see what it could be.

It turned out to be a four-yard-tall snowman looming over her.

Eyes and mouth made of coal, a carrot nose.

Its branch-like arms clutched a sack, and there was a red hat on its head.

"Whoa!"

This was an event monster—and the one that gave the *most* points to boot.

"You're mine!"

She spun around, unloading directly in the snowman's face.

Her bullets went all the way through, but the HP bar hardly budged.

And the snowman pushed right through her volley, swinging the sack at her.

"Eep? *That's* how it attacks?!"

The swing caught her on the shieldless side, shattering her cannons and sending her flying.

"Is this one of those magic-only monsters? Time to find out!"

She raised her shield and aimed her cannons diagonally down, shooting herself toward the snowman.

Devour tore away a huge chunk of the snowman's body, and she shot right through the gap left behind.

She landed with her usual lack of finesse, shattering a few more weapons, and spun around—only to find the HP bar still almost completely full.

"They sure are coming up with loads of new monster types... Hydra!"

At the least, it wasn't fast on its feet. The snowman didn't even try to dodge the attack, which hit dead center, splashing patches of poison everywhere.

"Wait...n-no effect at all?"

The attack itself did knock off a dot or two of HP, but the status effect didn't take hold or seem to do anything.

She could probably keep chipping away at it and win eventually, but it was clearly not worth the time.

"Still, I'd hate to let it get away..."

Weathering a storm of icicles the snowman was shooting at her, she considered her next move.

After a short while, she decided her only option was to team up with Syrup and take the slow-but-steady route.

"All ready!"

She used Giganticize to ride Syrup to a safe height and then blasted Spirit Cannon down at her target.

Meanwhile, she planned to burn through all her remaining uses of Hydra and then switch to her armaments.

"Okay! Hydra!"

Another poison dragon chewed through the snow—and this time, *all* its HP vanished.

"Huh? What the—?"

The monster vanished in a burst of light as something fell to the ground.

"Um…hmm. Oh! It must've been the instant death thing!"

This was the first time her Bug Urn Curse had activated, but it clearly worked like a charm.

Maple ran over to the item lying on the snow.

It was a box wrapped in red paper with a green ribbon, which really stood out against the white backdrop.

She scooped it up and checked the description.

Gift Box

Usable for a week after December 25. Contents are random.

"I wonder what's inside? Something Christmassy, I hope?"

Since her goal here was already accomplished, Maple headed back to town, thoroughly satisfied.

◆□◆□◆□◆□◆

Meanwhile, Sally was taking the opposite approach—running pell-mell across the map, slaughtering every event monster she could find, and racking up points.

After polishing off another group, she sheathed her daggers and decided on a quick rest.

"*Sigh…* I just can't catch up," she muttered.

She was picturing a certain friend she had invited to the game.

This was the first time she and Maple had played together for any length of time, and she loved that, but it also brought out her competitive streak.

And no matter what tactics she used, she couldn't picture herself ever taking Maple down.

"I never thought she'd get so strong…"

Maple was blazing a trail far out ahead of her, and Sally was hunting high and low for skills that might help, even scouring forums in her desperate bid to catch up. Sadly, she still hadn't discovered anything decisive.

"I'm not giving up, though. Back to the grind."

She forced her legs to start moving again.

Sword Dance was providing its maximum buff, and that meant Sally could dispatch the low-point monsters without even breaking stride, so she was making excellent progress.

"You guys should learn from Maple and boost your defense!"

Red sparks sprayed in her wake.

Just as monsters without piercing damage never stood a chance against Maple, foes with no AOEs couldn't even touch Sally.

"If she was *just* tanky, I could have taken Maple on, too."

She could handle these simplistic foes even with her mind elsewhere, but there were limits to how far raw talent could carry her, and she kept running into the same walls.

"Any good skills just lying around?"

After spending another two or three hours grinding the event, she spotted a huge snowman ahead of her.

"Oh, that's the high-point one. Lucky me."

Sally closed in, ducking under its swing and casting a spell.

"Fire Ball!"

Her magic wasn't that powerful, but this thing was especially weak against fire, and that sealed its fate.

Maple may have struggled with this monster, but a few Fire Balls was all it ordinarily took.

"Mm, delicious points!"

She had plenty of drops to collect before this event ended, so she was soon on the move once more.

The increasingly pressing need for some new power-up had her even more motivated than before.

Maple was too close to ignore, and Sally was too competitive to accept defeat.

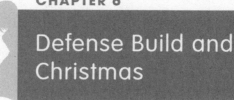

CHAPTER 6

Defense Build and Christmas

As Christmas drew near, Maple was looking forward to opening her Gift Box. It was beautifully wrapped, and she'd taken it out of her inventory just to stare at it.

"I wonder what's inside."

After a few more minutes, she double-checked the admin news to see when this event would officially end.

As she was reading, something in the article gave her an idea. She put the present away and bounded up from her chair.

Her feet took her directly to Iz's workshop.

She peered inside and found the master hard at work.

"Oh, Maple! What's up?"

"Um, it's not *super* important..."

Maple proceeded to suggest cooking up something Christmassy. Why? So they could have a party.

"Nice," Iz said. "But wait, I think tomorrow's the last day everyone can play until after Christmas."

"Would you need more time than that?"

"*That's* not the problem. It's a perfect chance for me to strut

my stuff! Now that I don't even need to repair Kasumi's weapon…
Well, I'm just glad to have a chance to do something else."

Iz wasn't just a blacksmith—she was a *crafter*.

"But if we're going to have a party, we'll want everyone there,
right? That means we've gotta be ready by then."

"R-right…and there's nobody else here…"

Maple and Iz were the only guild members logged in today.
Any party prep would have to be handled by the two of them.

"We'll need to gather a bunch of stuff to pull it off. Anything
you particularly want to eat?"

Maple showed Iz the admin e-mail she'd been looking at.

Iz knew what it said, so she quickly started nodding to herself.

"Right, the event monsters drop those Gift Boxes if you're lucky,
but their 'bad' drops actually come in handy for our purposes."

The common drops could be used to make cakes and chicken.
They weren't exactly valuable items, but it was definitely in the
spirit of the holiday. At least…the Japanese version.

"Heh-heh-heh… I'll go get us some!"

"Well, the drop rate still isn't exactly generous, and we're gonna
need a lot, so…good luck?"

"I got this!"

"That's the spirit. I'll take stock of the fruit and vegetables I'm
growing."

Iz waved her out, and Maple left the Guild Home.

She made her way to the town entrance and did a few stretches
to get herself fired up.

"Okay! Let's see how many I can get! It'd be nice to nab some
presents while I'm at it! Atrocity!"

Maple was enveloped in darkness and emerged in monster
form. Adroitly moving all her limbs, she scuttled off across the
snow.

* * *

A short run later, she encountered several event monsters.

Maple started every fight by breathing fire, roasting them instantly. Once the dust settled, she checked to see if they'd dropped anything.

"Snow Shards...these sell for a decent price, but you can't eat them. Hmm, I'll sell them later!"

Undaunted, she went looking for more monsters. The higher the point value, the better the drop rate. Consequently, she was especially looking for rarer monsters.

"Sally was absolutely right: Fire makes it easy!"

Maple ran around for a bit, scanning the horizon as she went. She was finding fewer monsters than she'd hoped.

She kept this up for a while but didn't run into many more and hadn't found anything she was looking for, either.

"...W-were they always this rare? Urgh, now what? It's looking less doable by the second..."

Feeling tired, she decided to curl up under a tree and rest, hoping to recover her motivation.

"...I wish the snow was deeper."

There was only a light dusting on the ground, not even enough for your feet to sink in. Maple thought it was a bit of a waste.

"Maybe there'll be a whole stratum like that someday..."

Then she and Sally could explore it together. After a moment imagining the adventures they'd have, she finally felt like resuming her drop hunt.

"Up and at 'em!" she cried, scrambling back to her feet. "Mm? Isn't that...?"

She saw someone in the distance she recognized, so she ran over.

And nobody ever missed Maple in monster form. They looked rather alarmed.

"Mii! Fancy meeting you here."

"Maple! Uh…" Mii coughed, then narrowed her eyes. "What's seems to be the matter? Did you need something?"

She had three guild members with her—Misery, Shin, and Marx, all of whom were trying not to stare.

"Not really! I was just out looking for event monsters and thought I'd say hi!"

"Oh…," Shin said, relaxing a bit. "Seeing you run up in that body, we just…naturally brace ourselves."

"Yes, I may never get used to it…"

"Humans should look human…"

Oblivious to this general air of discomfort, Maple kept casually talking to Mii.

"I just can't seem to find any! I checked places where there were lots before, but…"

"Mm? Oh, that won't work. The high-spawn areas change every day."

"They do?! Thaaat explains it."

Maple had not planned on participating in this event much, if at all, so she'd only just read the full message explaining how the event worked earlier that day. She never got past the part about the various ingredients.

"Whether you need it or not, it's always better to be in the know. It's something worth remembering."

"Mm, fair enough. I'll bear that in mind! Oh, right, Mii, if you're going monster hunting, can I tag along? You can have the Gift Boxes. Please!"

The trio with Mii looked puzzled. The presents were what everyone else was after.

"If you don't want those, why hunt at all? I mean, there's the points, but…it doesn't sound like you care about that."

"Um, actually…"

Maple explained her goal, and Shin looked taken aback by the very concept.

"That way of playing is basically alien to Shin."

"This guy…he barely bothered to put a table and a chair in his guild room…"

"I mean…I'm just here to fight, you know?"

"I say we team up," Misery said. "No reason to turn her down. Mii said you made it easy for her to go wild."

No one doubted Maple's fighting skills.

And if the price of her help was the dropped ingredients, well, that was a great bargain.

"Sounds like a plan. Maple, do you mind?"

"In this body, I'm pretty fast! Hop aboard!"

She flattened herself out, letting the others scramble on.

"Oh! I kinda wanted to try this!" Shin yelled, excitedly climbing on.

Marx was far more cautious. "It's not a ride," he grumbled. "You won't drop us, right?"

"Mii, shall we?"

"But of course."

Once all four were on board, Maple got up. Marx sat at her head.

"I'll show the way…so run where I point."

"Will do!"

Following his instructions, Maple raced across the field, and they were soon at their destination. The snow was falling pretty hard—a sure sign the spawn rates were higher here.

Maple put the others down, then activated Martyr's Devotion. They'd formed an ad hoc party, so as long as everyone stayed in range, death was nigh impossible.

"Seeing that form with angel wings is even creepier!"

"Yeah…some things are better off left unseen. I'm gonna go that way."

Marx walked off, setting some traps as he went.

"Flame Formation…here, and here…and maybe here?"

While he was getting set up, Shin used Splinter Sword to break his blade apart, and Misery imbued the shards with the fire element. And Mii was, of course, a fire specialist.

"Time to rock and roll. The monsters are spawning."

All that fruitless searching Maple had done, and now there were tons of them.

She was about to breathe fire herself, but before she could, Shin's blades, wreathed in fire, sliced apart a snowman monster.

Anything that got past those was burned by flames spurting out of Marx's traps.

"Mii, wanna see who beats the most?"

"You've got me on numbers. But if we make it total damage dealt…"

Their idle chitchat didn't make them any less ruthlessly efficient. Monster after monster kept dropping.

The field was awash in flames, damage sparks, and the lights of dying foes.

"If we don't need to defend or heal you, there's not much for me and Marx to do."

"Yep…nothing gets close."

"Wow! I wish I could make swords fly or cast big fire spells!"

"You're terrifying enough, Maple…"

"I love the angel wings."

"Heh-heh-heh. Next time we meet, I'll have mastered fire!"

"That's… Could you not try too hard?"

"I'm looking forward to seeing that."

"Misery?!"

And while they bantered, more monsters went up in flames.

They repeated this operation in a few more places, tearing through the monster population and getting Maple all the ingredients she needed.

"Well, Maple? That enough?"

"Eh-heh-heh! Totally. Thanks, Mii!"

"You helped us plenty, too. We didn't have to run from place to place on foot or worry about defending ourselves. It was a blast!"

"Well, see you around...hopefully in...a human body, next time..."

"Bye now. I do hope you enjoy your feast."

Maple waved and headed back to her guild.

"If we end up with extra, I should share with Mii's group."

She reverted to human form near town and ran back home.

The next day...

Maple Tree members gathered in their Guild Home's hall. On the table were the fruits of Iz's labor: roast chicken, ice cream cake, salad, and soup.

"Um...S-Sally? Wh-what am I supposed to say here?" Maple asked in a panic.

"Huh? You actually stood up without a plan?!"

"Augh...! Merry Christmas! And a happy New Year!"

Everyone cheered and promptly dug into Iz's feast.

"Well, I'm pretty proud of what I managed to do! And once this event wraps up, we may not see these ingredients for a while... such a shame."

""It's all great!""

The twins were both stuffing their faces, as were Chrome and Kasumi.

"Always nice to take a break from the grind."

"Yes, it's a nice change of pace. The most important thing is to have fun."

"So where *did* you get that katana? It must've been a weird quest, right?"

"…That's top secret."

"Figured. Well, I'm looking forward to seeing it in action, even if that shrinking effect is a little weird."

"Ugh, spare me…and then there's the sarashi…"

While they talked, Iz gave Kanade a new puzzle, which took him all of one minute to solve.

"Well…the food's good, so eat up!" she said. It mostly sounded like she was making excuses for the puzzle.

"G-got it. I'll have some more now!"

"The next one'll be twice as hard!"

"Mm, can't wait."

Kanade took a big bite.

"Mm! With all you've made for me, I'm gonna gather materials for you. It's guaranteed that anything I give you will come back better."

Maple and Sally were listening to the merry festivities, looking delighted.

"Was it hard putting all this together?"

"I had help, so everything worked out. Wish I'd thought of it sooner!"

"When I logged in and saw you partied up, I almost freaked out! But I guess I'm getting used to you surprising me."

"Yeah?"

"Yeah, I mean… You're pretty much *always* doing something unexpected."

She named a few examples, and they were basically all skills Maple had stumbled across.

"Eh-heh-heh. I was just having fun, and before I knew it, this is how it turned out!"

"Yup! I'm content as long as you're enjoying yourself."

Maple turned toward Sally, smiling. "Sally, next year will be even *more* fun."

"Can't wait to play more with ya!"

And the party went on strong till all the food was gone.

On Christmas Day...

Maple was finally able to open the Gift Box she'd found.

She and Sally both showed up in the Guild Home at the same time.

"Oh, Sally! I didn't know you'd be here."

"Could say the same about you, Maple. You planning on going anywhere?"

"Mm...I don't think so. I'm mostly here for my present. Basically just couldn't wait to open it."

Maple took the red box out of her inventory.

"You got one? So did I."

Sally's present was yellow. The wrapping was a little different, but it was undoubtedly the same Gift Box drop item.

She held it in both hands, letting the emotions wash over her.

"It was a long journey," she said, stroking the lid. "I lost count of how many I defeated."

Maple decided *not* to mention she'd got hers the first time she fought one.

She decided to forge ahead instead. "Let's crack them open! I'm dying to see what's inside!"

Both tugged the ribbons and popped the lids off. Inside each was a scroll.

The items that gave you new skills.
"A skill, huh? Let's see what's what."
They checked the skill descriptions.

Ice Pillar

Creates a single indestructible column of ice for 3MP.
Limit five.
Lasts one minute.

Zone Freeze

For three seconds after activation, immobilizes any players or monsters in contact with the ground within a five-yard radius of the user.
Three-minute cooldown.

The first was Sally's scroll.
The second was Maple's.
"Sally, look what I got!"
"Here's mine. Looks like there are several types. I haven't used Oceanic much lately, so this might be more useful... Gotta watch my MP, though."
Sally was muttering away, figuring out what this new skill meant for her.
If she used it right, it could definitely help with her defenses.
"Meanwhile, I can just freeze any monsters that seem strong! I just go *schiiing!*"
"Yeah, that sounds good."
"Yep, yep. I guess that's it for this year!"
"Mm? Really?"

Maple already had her logout window open.

"I gotta pick away at our homework, and the start of January's always really hectic. I think I might not be back on for a bit. Sally, don't wait until the last minute to do the homework."

"I already did it all, so I'm actually gonna be playing a ton."

Sally's motivation levels could make a *big* difference. Shaking her head at that, Maple logged out.

Left to her own devices, Sally returned to planning.

"They're gonna add another new stratum soon, so things are quiet for now… We haven't found a way to weaken the dude behind the last gate, so I can't do that… I guess I could backtrack and explore more around the machine town?"

When Maple wasn't around, Sally was usually trying to catch up, so it was rare for her to be operating without a specific goal like this.

"Maybe following my whims once in a while won't hurt. It works for Maple!"

Pinning her hopes on the upcoming fifth stratum, Sally headed back to the third.

Ultimately, she found no new skills and no weird events.

All she really got out of it was a solid grasp on how to use Ice Pillar.

But that was enough to prove just how useful her new skill was.

All along, she'd handled AOE threats with magic barriers, but these didn't last long.

Having something that stuck around for a full minute was an enormous boon.

Part of her wished it wasn't translucent—she was fully visible behind it—but even so, it was still pretty great.

CHAPTER 7

Defense Build to the Fifth Stratum

Maple and Sally's winter break came to an end, and before long, they were halfway through January.

It was the moment Sally had been waiting for—the launch of the fifth stratum.

On the day in question, Sally might have been the first to arrive at their Guild Home, but every other member soon joined her.

"Oh, everyone's here!"

She hadn't expected that and was as delighted as she was surprised.

"Mm? Wait, but not Maple?" Chrome asked.

"Yeah, Maple…," Sally said sheepishly. "She's got the flu. Again. Happens *every* year."

"O-oh. Then do we want to save it for a later date?" he suggested.

They discussed it but concluded that Maple could easily get through it by pairing up with whoever happened to be around, so they should forge ahead while everyone else was present.

No one objected.

Frankly, odds were Maple could solo the boss.

And so Maple Tree headed into the dungeon leading to the fifth stratum without her.

The seven of them were making short work of the monsters on the way to the dungeon.

Chrome pulled the aggro while Mai and Yui hit back hard. That was all it took. Chrome made sure nothing even came close to attacking the twins. Maple tended to overshadow him, but he was a top-class great shielder in his own right.

The main effect of Maple's absence was that the party's top speed was whatever the twins' Agility-free builds could manage. But otherwise, they made for a very solid party.

"Oh, there it is!" Chrome said, warding off a monster blow. He pointed at a cave yawning open up ahead.

"Let's beat this thing," Kanade said, bookshelves dancing overhead.

"Can't wait!"

They plunged straight into the dungeon itself.

The interior was filled with monsters that either nullified or resisted physical damage.

If they were only resistant, the twins could still one-shot them, but if they completely canceled it out, that wouldn't fly. And there were a great deal of wisps and spectral monsters, which had a negative impact on Sally's performance. This meant Kanade and Kasumi were up, and they took point as Maple Tree traversed the dungeon.

Iz didn't really fight much, but she'd done her fair share of exploring on the fourth stratum and had learned a few tricks to deal with this kind of foe.

Chrome, too, had fought endless wisps; it was easy for him to anticipate their flames and block them, buying time for Kanade to take them out.

If he took damage, Iz's items could easily fix that.

And the trash mobs that only *resisted* were never a threat in the first place.

This team could easily steamroll a dungeon full of monsters even without Maple.

They reached the boss door without breaking a sweat.

"Should I?" Sally asked, jerking her thumb at the door. Everyone nodded, bracing for the impending battle.

As the doors swung open, everyone leaped in.

Deep inside the room was a nine-tailed fox sporting sleek yellow fur, each of its tails swaying.

"Stick to the plan!" Sally yelled, and the party scattered.

Sally shot forward and hung left while Kasumi and Kanade weaved right.

The other three stayed by the door, safely behind Chrome.

As they ran, Sally and Kasumi both used the items Iz had given them—yellow crystals, which they crushed with their hands. This made their weapons crackle with yellow light.

The crystals had applied a paralysis effect to their weapons—a highly effective tactic against quick enemies like this fox.

"Eyes on me!" Sally yelled, slashing its foreleg and drawing its aggro. It predictably came after her, biting, slashing, and using its tails in an attempt to sweep her feet out from under her, but she made excellent use of her new Ice Pillar to avoid those attacks and hit back with counters.

And while she dodged this flurry, Kasumi and Kanade could do whatever they wanted.

* * *

"Paralyze Bomb!"

"Fourth Blade: Whirlwind!"

Kanade's spell and Kasumi's four-hit combo also had paralysis effects.

Sally kept laying on the damage, keeping the heat off them. When all was said and done, the fox *was* designed to be weak to paralysis, so it didn't take long for it to lock up.

"Paralysis active!"

It would be a lot harder to inflict the status effect a second time, so this was their one shot.

But with Mai and Yui on their side, one shot was all they needed.

Chrome had kept their ultimate weapon safe from any stray shock waves, but now they came running out, headed right at the fox.

Each step they took was like a countdown to the boss's death.

""Double Stamp!""

Their hammers swung, each delivering two titanic blows that ignored all future boss phases, sounding the funeral bells.

With the twins on their team, they could invalidate all the design team's efforts. And if their absent guild master were here, they could watch all phases play out without them mattering at all.

◆□◆□◆□◆□◆

A few days after everyone else made it to the fifth stratum, Maple arrived at the fourth stratum Guild Home and found only Sally there.

"Everyone's upstairs?"

"Yup. Need any help? I don't have much time today, so if I'm coming, we should make it quick."

She definitely seemed like she was in a hurry, so Maple decided to appreciate the thought and let her log out.

"Oh, before you go—how was it? Strong, or...?"

"Uh...well, definitely one of the strongest enemies on this floor."

"Really?! Um, but you soloed it, right?"

"......? No, all seven of us went. But I'm sure you can manage on your own."

"Oh yeah? You can all work together now?"

Maple beamed, looking immensely pleased by that.

"Yeah? Sure. Sorry I'm not helping today. If I didn't have prior plans..."

"Don't worry about it! I'll be fine. You said I would be! And I'm sure I will be, too."

Maple said her good-byes and headed out.

"She just had to go the moment she got over the flu, huh? Hmm. Either way, I gotta run!"

Sally logged out, not wanting to miss her real-world plans.

Maple ran straight for her destination. Everyone was ahead of her now, and she was eager to catch up.

"It's showtime!"

She took a deep breath and stepped into the boss room.

"Hellooo?"

"Oh...? I did not expect a *human*," the tall white-clad ruler said.

Maple was here to face the *strongest foe*.

"Heh-heh-heh! You're gonna let me reach the fifth stratum!" she declared.

She followed him onto the circle, into the battle zone.

"Shall we begin, human?" the ruler said. In his right hand was a naginata over two yards long.

"Don't be too hard, please! Full Deploy! Predators!"

There was a *clang*, and an instant later, Maple's body was bristling with artillery.

She had a shield on her left and a massive machine sword on her right, completely hiding her body from view.

"Commence Assault!"

A barrage of cannon fire and lasers filled the air.

The volume of fire was so high that she only had to aim in a general direction.

Unfortunately, the ruler deflected every bullet with his blade, cutting them right out of the air.

But since Maple's attacks never slowed for a second, he also couldn't attack her.

"You fight like Sally! Syrup, Giganticize!"

She had her pet float up above, and she and her monsters moved closer to the ruler.

This decreased the interval between each fired round, but still, the ruler remained unharmed.

"Syrup, Spirit Cannon!"

A beam of light shot down from above—and the ruler dodged it.

"Urgh...Hydra!"

Poison surged out of her, bearing down on her foe.

In response, the ruler spun his naginata so fast that it sent all the poison spraying away harmlessly.

But an instant later, Maple rocketed in, her all-consuming shield and dully gleaming sword both thrust forward, turning herself into a living bullet.

But this also provided a momentary lapse in the cover fire.

"Farewell, human!"

The ruler's reaction took advantage of the lull. His naginata sliced into Maple's weapons before sending her and her monsters flying.

The shield and sword undoubtedly made contact with the ruler's body, but they left nothing more than a flesh wound.

"Yikes! Whoa! Whoa!"

Maple bounced across the ground a few times, clanking loudly, and scrambled to her feet.

And found the ruler right on top of her.

"Saturating Chaos!"

The monster lunged at the ruler, but he neatly dodged it.

However, her Predators were right behind, and their mouths closed around both his arms.

This seemingly did nothing to slow his naginata; his counter-attack cut through them both.

Maple came charging in through the shower of damage sparks, swinging her great shield and slamming into the ruler's right side with Devour.

"You got my Predators, but I can't tell if that was piercing damage!"

If she used Martyr's Devotion, she'd lose a lot of HP. If piercing damage high enough to take down both Predators hit her then, there was a good chance she'd die instantly. Better safe than sorry.

Maple was definitely getting better at gaming in general. She understood that she could and should use different tactics when fighting on her own versus when she was working with other guild members. She redeployed the damaged weapons and took aim at the ruler.

"Commence Assault!"

As her barrage resumed, she caught her breath.

"He's got a lot of attacks, but I still haven't taken damage, so if I keep this up, I should be okay, I think."

Maple was so ludicrously strong, it was hard to tell which of them was the boss.

He was still batting aside everything she fired at him, but she could see his HP bar, and the hits she'd landed had whittled him down a bit, with *maybe* 80 percent remaining.

"Once more...!"

But as she took a step forward, the ruler changed his attack pattern.

He made a leap that took him well outside the barrage's range. Five yards high, he soared, purple flames fanning out around him.

"Eep?!"

Maple quickly tried to turn, but the flames shot forward first.

"Allow me to reciprocate," the ruler said.

Every skill she'd used was being reproduced with fire.

With an ordinary great shielder, this skill would have resulted in a close-quarters counter—but with Maple, the flames shot out from afar and scorched the earth, blinding her.

Waves of heat, exploding firebolts, and dragons made of fire all came rushing in.

"Augh! Wh-what's going on?!"

Maple didn't have any attacks with a piercing effect, so she wasn't taking damage, but as the inferno rose higher than her head, she also couldn't see much of anything.

"F-for now, I'll just..."

She aimed her weapons down, using the self-destruct to propel herself above the ruler's flames, and headed to where Syrup waited.

"Martyr's Devotion!"

Angel wings unfurled through the tangle of weapons, and Maple's hair turned golden. She chugged a potion to restore the lost HP.

"Syrup!" she yelled, landing so hard it almost seemed like she might crack its shell.

The intense heat seared them both, but Martyr's Devotion kept Syrup safe from harm. After a short while, the flames on the ground died out enough that she was able to locate the ruler.

"He's copying me...?"

None of the skills Maple knew would actually work on her.

So as long as he was only mimicking her skills, she was *completely* safe.

"I think I'll just stay up here until this is over."

She plonked herself down on Syrup's back, ignoring the scalding heat.

When the fires were finally gone, she released Martyr's Devotion and jumped back down.

"Commence Assault!"

She began her barrage again, forcing the ruler back on the defensive as she steadily closed in on him.

Sword and shield high, she charged in a third time. They swept past each other. Maple's weapons and armor crumbled, but Devour chewed another chunk off the ruler.

But the damage she was taking was only to her weaponry.

And when her armor broke, it reformed. When her weapons broke, she redeployed.

"Okay, as long as I can keep this up!"

Maple righted herself and was about to turn toward him...

...until her eyes spotted a naginata hurtling at her, glowing red.

"Wah!"

She threw up her shield, but the naginata spun, striking her from a new angle.

The sideways sweep hit her hard and sent her flying.

"Urgh...unh! Commence Assault!"

When she stopped tumbling, she got to one knee, trying to keep him away.

Red sparks were shooting out of her side.

"Argh, piercing...potion! Potion!"

Scrambling, she pulled a potion out of her inventory and used it.

She'd been just below half health, but a single potion fully restored it.

A decently strong potion could easily refill HP to max when it was as low as Maple's.

"Hmm...he blocks all ranged attacks. What else can I do?"

Maple didn't really have many close-range attacks. Atrocity was certainly the most effective of these, but otherwise, she only had Devour, launching herself into the fray, and the Predators.

"Hmm...oh! Let's go with that."

Like before, she fired herself at him.

Once again, they shot past each other, with the same result.

"But now...!"

With an extra-big *bang*, Maple rocketed skyward.

A moment later, the ruler's naginata caught only air, and Maple landed safely on Syrup's back, high above.

"Whew. Thanks, Syrup! You're a lifesaver."

She gave her pet a pat on the shell and then hopped back down.

The instant she landed, she charged at the boss again, not letting him start any other attack routines.

Each time she charged, she took refuge on Syrup before coming back down for more. Looping this let her chip away at the boss's health without taking any damage.

*   *   *

Maple's barrage had kept the boss preoccupied to begin with, and by using herself as a cannonball, she could instantly become mobile in three dimensions in a way no other player could manage. The ruler had no way of defending against that.

His HP kept going down. Bit by bit.

She managed to get through half his total pool without letting him strike back.

"......!"

After yet another charge, she glanced down from Syrup's back and noticed a *change*.

"Most impressive, human!" the ruler bellowed as a swirling vortex of light appeared around him.

A wind picked up close to the ground. Maple could hear it begin howling.

This clear shift made her brace her shield, watching closely from above.

"Let's see how you handle *this*!"

The ruler began running—straight into the air above.

The light became a tail, trailing after him as he quickly closed the distance.

"You're kidding?!"

His naginata was wreathed in light, too. That was the telltale red glow of a piercing attack. Maple knew she was in trouble.

"Syrup! Rest!"

Syrup vanished back into her ring.

And without the flying support, she succumbed to gravity, dropping like a stone.

"Commence Assault!"

Firing to keep her distance, Maple headed back to ground level. Floating just above it, the ruler gave chase.

"Um…argh…! Oh, I know!"

She didn't need to change directions, so she opened her inventory mid-flight.

"There!"

Glowing objects rained down in her wake.

Potions from her inventory.

"Next…this way!"

She changed direction and scattered even more behind her.

So that the ground was blanketed in potions.

This way, she could grab one whenever she needed it.

They would only stay put for two hours, but any one of them could fully restore her health.

"Here goes!"

Summoning her courage, she turned back toward the ruler.

"Hah!"

She twisted herself, slamming shield and sword home—and soaked a vicious naginata slash to the shoulder, which sent her tumbling across the ground.

"Ow…can't let this go on for long."

That was her first taste of damage in a long while.

Maple very much preferred not feeling this kind of pain, so she quickly scooped up a potion and got rid of it.

If her foe was dishing out piercing damage, she wanted to wrap this fight up quick.

"One more time!"

Flames burst from her feet, and she rocketed skyward.

The ruler danced upward, wreathed in light.

Their two lights clashed together, burst, and sent red sparks flying.

Maple crashed to the ground, weapons shattering, and scooped up a potion.

"Another…?"

But something was wrong.

"My weapons…won't deploy?"

She'd been burning through them with each blastoff.
But there was a *limit*.
If the materials she'd poured into the skill ran out, she wouldn't be able to use them anymore.
And between her constant fusillades and taking flight multiple times, she had burned through that stock.
"You're through, human!"
No longer subjected to her barrage, the ruler rushed toward Maple, shooting missiles of fire and swinging his naginata.
"Atrocity!"
The monster form enveloped her.
Spraying damage effects, the ruler's arm and his naginata were swallowed by her gaping maw.
"Got him!"
Her claws raked his sides.
Both were taking and dealing damage.
When he hit 30 percent HP remaining, a massive shock wave freed him from Maple's mandibles.
As the ruler bounded away, the light gathered around him.
"We're not done yet, human!"
Then the ruler *expanded*, growing bigger and bigger, his white hair streaming freely behind him.

The two monsters hurtled toward each other, unleashing all their respective might.
If their fight so far had hinged on technique, now it was about brute strength.

Neither side attempted to evade; they simply did their best to match the other, blow for blow.

"Still here!" Maple yelled, her breath setting the ruler aflame.

His fists were glowing red, slamming into her sides.

And as his HP dropped below 20 percent...

"Urp...!"

The monster skin coating Maple crumbled, ejecting her onto the ground.

Atrocity might have boosted her attack, but it was still no match for the ruler's power.

And his hail of piercing blows had torn her monstrous skin away before she could down him.

"Hydra! Syrup, Awaken! Giganticize!"

She called her pet out once more and warded off the ruler's approach with a burst of poison.

Her opponent was no longer dodging; he tanked the damage and still came at her swinging.

"Saturating Chaos! ...Argh, Syrup, Mother Nature!"

Maple was throwing out every skill she could think of to slow him down. Syrup's skill created massive vines that bought her enough time to scramble up onto the shell and fly away.

"Gotta hurry...augh?!"

She'd just looked down.

The ruler's fist punched through the vine barrier and then promptly fired a fist-sized bullet of wind.

"Syrup!"

It struck her pet head-on, one-shotting it and dropping Maple to the ground.

Even as she fell, the ruler thrust his fist toward her.

She just happened to be holding her shield in the right place at the right angle and blocked the blow—but in midair, she had no way to stand her ground.

This was far beyond ordinary knockback. She was sent flying, though she took no damage.

Maple was fundamentally skill-reliant and wasn't very good at protecting herself. There was no guarantee she could block the next attack.

Before she could even get up, she saw the ruler charging her once more.

If he got to her, she had no way of putting distance between them again.

But her eyes caught something on the ground in front of her—which gave her an idea.

"Quick Change!"

Blue light coated her, and in the blink of an eye, her gear was all white.

"Next..."

She scooped up the potions scattered nearby, topping up her increased HP pool.

By that point, the ruler's fist was inches away.

"Aegis!"

White light overwhelmed the red damage sparks, covering her in a dome of light.

Flawless protection would nullify every attack Maple took during the next ten seconds.

"Come on...go down!"

She threw out every skill she had, trying to rack up the damage.

The ruler's HP was finally down to 10 percent, but even as poison gushed from her short sword, Maple was starting to panic.

Once Aegis ended, she essentially had no defensive or offensive skills left.

The ruler's flurry of attacks was too fast and would not grant her enough time to use Hydra again.

She had no way of surviving this, she thought—but then the name of a skill floated into her mind. One she'd tucked away in a corner and forgotten all about.

"Oh! There *is* one left!"

The effects of Aegis ended even as she spoke, and the ruler's next attack bore down upon her.

"Zone Freeze!"

The skill she'd earned in the last event. It stopped foes around her in their tracks.

An extension of light. Three seconds of pure gold.

Time enough for her to use that forgotten skill.

"Break Core!"

A hole opened up over Maple's heart, and a small sphere emerged, pulsing with a reddish light.

It stopped in the air two yards from her.

Five more seconds until activation.

Indomitable Guardian kicked in, allowing her to withstand the particularly powerful final hit of his combo. Maple snatched up another potion, using it. These had really made all the difference here. But that, too, was bittersweet.

Then—on opposing sides of the sphere, Maple and the ruler were lifted up, as if freed from the constant pull of gravity. Then they began to *orbit*.

"Ruler, I'm sure this will count as a draw. But I absolutely have to get to the fifth stratum, so I *will* be back!"

This was a Machine God skill.

The only one not fueled by her equipment.

Maple had forgotten it for a reason. This skill was fundamentally a self-destruct technique.

The skill description had said it would prevent the use of attacks in range and would deal massive damage to user and target alike. That description—particularly the idea of self-destructing—had been enough to banish it from Maple's mind.

"Bye!"

Maple closed her eyes, waiting for death's embrace. A moment later, a pillar of flames pierced the heavens, consuming Maple with it.

"Argh, so frustrating!" Maple muttered, lying flat on the ground with her eyes closed.

She was so worn out that she felt ready to sleep right then and there. Losing bothered her more than she'd ever expected.

"I'm done! I'm logging out for the day."

She opened her eyes, pushing herself upright.

"Wait...why am I...?"

She was still in the battle zone.

And the ruler she'd been fighting lay sprawled out at her feet.

"Mm-hmm? Hmm. But why?"

She was absolutely certain she'd blown herself up. But for some reason, she still had half her health left.

"My defense kicked in? Oh. Ohhh! Heh-heh! See? I knew defense is the best!"

Delighted by the fact that her overwhelming tankiness had saved her, she turned to the defeated ruler.

"Um, are you okay?"

She knelt down, poking him until he sat up.

"Ha-ha-ha! Nicely done, human!" he guffawed.

Dusting himself off, the ruler rose to his feet.

"Come with me," he said as he stalked away. Maple obediently trotted after him.

He stepped onto a new magic circle, and they both were taken back into the highest room on the fourth stratum.

"Now then, human. As promised, I dub thee my successor. That is your goal here, yes?"

His hands began to glow, and two crimson vessels appeared— shallow cups for drinking sake.

He handed one to Maple and summoned a large gourd-shaped jug, filling both their cups.

"I never thought it would be a human. Your kind are unable to consume our liquor, so this is not real sake, but it will have to do."

"Uh, fine by me!"

They both drank, and Maple acquired a new skill.

"Skill: Pandemonium I acquired."

The ruler spoke a while longer, and Maple made listening noises. Eventually, he wrapped things up.

"I'm sure you have places to go. But do come again! You are always welcome here. As long as I still breathe, I would be more than happy to fight you again."

"Um. I definitely don't want to fight, but sure, I'll swing by sometimes!"

She waved and quickly left the room. Once the sliding door was closed, she finally allowed herself to stretch.

"Whew... Ow. I'm so tired! I've had enough fighting to last me a while."

She'd taken a lot of damage in that battle and was completely exhausted even though she'd won.

Maple didn't even want to engage in *easy* combat for a while.

"Oh, right. I should check that skill. Let's see..."

Pandemonium I

For one minute, summon a red and a blue ogre.
The ogres' stats depend on their skill levels.
While active, the user's skills are all sealed. Equipment skills are not affected.

Maple checked both ogres' current stats and then frowned.

"Um, so if it's at level I...how do I raise it?"

She could only think of one way.

The ruler had *just* said he'd fight her again as long as he still drew breath.

That was clearly it.

She would have to beat him. Again and again.

"Yikes," Maple said. "In that case, I don't care."

The words slipped out unbidden. She definitely had no plans to battle the ruler again anytime soon.

She left the building and headed back into town.

By that point, her mind had started working again, prompting a vital question.

"Why aren't I on the next stratum?!"

Her yell of horror echoed across the streets around.

CHAPTER 8

Defense Build and Cloud Town

"I wanna get to the fifth stratum, but howww?!"

Maple didn't want to fight again today, so she flopped down on a bench at the center of town. Then she saw a party of six coming her way, with a familiar face in the middle.

"Frederica?"

"Mm, Maple? What's up?"

Since she was fighting Sally on the regular, Frederica wound up talking to Maple surprisingly often.

So when Maple called out to her, she naturally stopped for a chat.

Maple was totally confused about why she was still stuck on this stratum but figured Frederica might know the answer. She decided to ask.

"Augh…it was a mistake?! All that for…a mistake?!"

The truth left her in a deflated heap on the bench again.

"The six of us are headed for the dungeon leading upstairs. We'll have to play together some other time."

"Oh…oh? Then…"

Maple slowly got back to her feet.

"Can I tag along? I can keep everyone safe...really, that's *all* I can do right now."

She quickly explained that she'd used up the bulk of her skills.

"Hmm? Um...why not? We've got room in the party."

Frederica couldn't see any reason to turn the offer down.

It was like adding a secret boss to your party to beat the normal one.

And who could object to a guaranteed victory?

"Then let's do it!"

Maple joined their party, and they headed out right after.

Unfortunately, she was stuck moving at turtle speeds. Possibly even slower.

"It might be better if we just carry you," Frederica said. She buffed herself, picked white-winged Maple up, and then sped off toward the dungeon.

"I'll handle all the defense!"

"That's all we ask."

Maple's mere presence was enough to ensure everyone's safety. They faced no threats on the road.

Naturally, that meant all seven of them reached the boss room in peak condition.

"Stick together!"

They closed ranks in front of Maple and advanced as one.

The fourth event had proven just how crucial Martyr's Devotion could be, and most players knew full well it could make anyone in her party functionally immortal.

There was no need to spread out and divide the boss's attention—Maple simply neutralized all its attacks, leaving them free to commit everything to a frontal assault.

They chipped away at the fox's health, driving it into a corner. Everyone in Frederica's team was a skilled player, so Maple's support was all they needed.

"Agh, it's getting faster!" Frederica yelled.

The boost was dramatic.

The front-liners were no longer able to keep up with it, and their attacks started consistently missing.

The fox's HP was below the 20 percent mark, but if they couldn't land any more hits...

"It's not as bad as Sally, but still...," Frederica muttered, her spells never letting up.

Some of these were hitting, but everyone could tell this would take ages.

The fox leaped back again, and Frederica sighed.

"What a hass—?!"

Fighting Sally had taught her a few things.

It helped hone her sense for the kind of hunches Dread always talked about.

And the one she just felt told her something *bad* was coming up behind.

She spun around.

"Pandemonium!"

Maple's golden locks shifted back to black, and her wings lost their light.

They were replaced with fire.

Maple was now backlit by a purple inferno.

Behind it, a parade of demons appeared. A giant ogre stood on either side of Maple.

She led the procession, which looked like a march of nightmares.

"Go!"

The ogres lunged forward, clubs raised high.

The fox had nowhere to run.

Each ogre was every bit as massive as the boss, and they had it boxed in.

Their stats were still on the low side, so they couldn't fell the fox with a single blow.

Instead, they just kept pounding away. Blow after blow rained down, delivered from towering heights.

Frederica's eyes went wide as the air filled with red sparks.

The damage effects sprayed from the fox like gushing blood.

Speed boosts were no use if there was no space to run.

And few things were more futile than trying to escape when every step meant certain doom.

By the time the fox was dead, Frederica's team looked almost meditative.

When the lights marking its demise faded, the path to the fifth stratum finally opened.

"Thanks, Frederica! Lemme know if you need help with anything else! Later!"

"......Uh, yeah... Will do...," Frederica managed to say, trying to shake off her trance. By the time she did, Maple was already gone.

"Where'd Maple go? Oh, upstairs. Right."

Frederica tried to think, then gave up and turned to the player next to her.

"Any clue what that skill was?"

Her brain was slowly starting to move again. Even as she asked the question, one answer sprang to mind.

"Oh...the white ogre, huh?"

"Did she find a way to weaken it?"

"Maybe not. I mean...we *are* talking about Maple..."

For all they knew, she could've taken it on at full power.

Maple had earned enough trust that nobody required proof.

They knew how strong she was, so this was just the logical conclusion.

◆□◆□◆□◆□◆

"Fifth stratum, here I am!"

Maple stepped onto the fifth stratum a few days after the rest of her guild.

The ground was spotlessly white and, surprisingly, a bit springy.

It was a land made of clouds. A paradise in the heavens.

"It's fluffier than my bed!"

Enjoying the spring beneath her steps, Maple headed for her Guild Home.

"So this is the fifth-stratum town!"

Behind a wall of clouds was a town so white, it hurt her eyes.

No real-world walls or roads could ever be this unblemished. But a glance at a nearby home soon proved not *everything* was made of soft clouds.

"This bit definitely isn't."

She poked the wall of the home to be sure and discovered it was all smooth.

It felt more like polished marble than anything else. Not springy at all.

"Well, if we can stand on clouds, this stratum ought to have some interesting materials."

Wondering what sort of items a stratum like this would have, she pressed on, checking her map occasionally—until she reached their Guild Home.

She opened the white door out front and stepped inside.

"Nobody home? Guess not. Then I'll log out for the day! I'm beat."

She pulled up her screen, deciding to take it easy for a while, and tapped the LOG OUT button.

A few days later...

Maple was talking to Sally in their Guild Home.

"Oh...that *was* a big mistake."

"Yeah... I've never been so tired."

"Mm. I *thought* our conversation wasn't adding up..."

"In hindsight, it totally wasn't."

Maple explained how she'd made it to the fifth stratum after the ogre fight.

And halfway through the story, she realized she'd shown another guild her new skill.

"I was too tired to think straight!"

"Well, it's not *too*, too terrible. It'll take more than that to really shock anyone at this point..."

In Sally's mind, Frederica was already convinced Maple could do literally anything, but she hadn't actually quite reached that level yet.

Sally herself already had one foot in that door, so she tended to assume everyone was on the same page, but in reality, it took being this close to Maple to truly appreciate the possibilities.

"I guess I won't worry about it too much, then. You go exploring yet, Sally?"

Sally thought for a second, then clapped her hands. "I haven't seen everything, but I've wandered around a bit. This map has an insane amount of verticality, and the field is full of hills and stairs. Also…"

"Also…what?"

"The ground feel changes up a lot, so it's easy to trip if you don't pay attention."

"Really? I'd better be careful."

"That sort of thing could literally be the death of me, so…"

Sally could handle furious blows and multiple enemies, but unsteady footing was a huge problem.

It meant making constant small adjustments or failing to evade in time.

"You want to see stuff now, Maple?"

"I dunno. I feel like I did a week's worth of fighting, so I'll save that for later."

"Sounds good. Best to enjoy things at your own speed. That way you don't burn yourself out. I'd rather you stick around for the long haul!"

That had been Sally's motivation from the beginning and would never change.

"Mm, I'm having fun."

"Glad to hear it. But I do wanna explore some more. If I see anything I think you'd like, I'll let you know."

Sally stood up and shot her a grin.

"Oh! Can't wait."

"I'll explore enough for the both of us, Maple!"

"You do that."

"Bye!"

"Have fun!"

And the door closed behind Sally.

*   *   *

"Ha-ha… She actually did it…"

Sally was leaning on the door, staring up at the skies above.

The clear blue reflected in her eyes.

She closed them, took a deep breath, and then started moving.

"I really don't like losing."

The gap had opened up again, and the only way to close it was to start running as fast as she could.

"I pull you in here, and then I get all competitive on my own… I do feel bad about that, you know?" she muttered to no one in particular.

The cloud-based ground had a great deal of ups and downs and wasn't great for running.

Even Sally could barely manage half her usual speed.

If she tried going any faster, she usually lost her balance and went tumbling down.

"Well, that looks worth scoping out."

A cloud loomed high in the air above, like a cumulonimbus in the summer sky. From down below, where Sally stood, a path leading upward into the cloud's interior was visible.

"Should I…? Yeah, I'm thinking yes."

She drew her draggers before stepping into the cumulonimbus.

Once she passed through the narrow entrance, the path branched.

On guard against ambushes, Sally cautiously began exploring the maze.

"Not seeing any traps or monsters…so far, so good."

She was tapping lots of walls and floors, picking her away along. Each time she reached a corner, she flattened herself against the wall, peeking around.

"Whoops."

There was a monster around this corner—a floating gray cloud. It looked like it was ready to rain.

"Oboro, Fleeting Shadow."

This skill made her momentarily invisible, and she used that to approach undetected, unleashing several dagger strikes at the perfect moment.

The monster's HP bar dropped like a brick. When she became visible again, it got ready to attack but its HP ran out *just* before it could lash out.

"Going solo is probably gonna start being a whole lot harder unless Sword Dance is constantly maxed out..."

She had to make quick work of her foes because otherwise the number of evasive actions she was forced to take would rise dramatically.

In other words, staying successfully dodgy meant she had to maintain a certain DPS.

But since reaching the fifth stratum, even with the Sword Dance buff max, it was taking her longer to kill enemies. Long enough that they could almost swing back.

The monsters were catching up with her stats.

"Which means I could really use a new skill. Hngg!"

Farther down the passage, she saw another cloud monster up ahead. This one was crackling with electricity.

"Interesting...so that last one's attacks were probably water?"

If the one she'd killed while cloaked had been a rain cloud, this one was a thunderhead.

"Let's see how big its AOE is."

Ready to backpedal at a moment's notice, she took a step closer.

As she moved into range, it generated smaller clouds, scattering them around itself.

"Yikes!"

Sally quickly bounded back, and a moment later, lightning started arcing between all the satellite clouds and the main one.

The surge died down after a few seconds.

Once she was sure of that, Sally used Leap to close in before relying on Double Slash and regular attacks to finish it off.

"Slow on the uptake. Definitely a trash enemy."

The warm-up had been so long that even Maple would probably have had time to dodge.

It covered a pretty broad range, but it was no threat to Sally.

Sally pressed on through the cloud passage, picking paths that went up.

She had a hunch the goal might be at the top of the cumulonimbus.

And she was right on the money.

"Oh, I'm out already?"

Bright blue skies opened up before her.

She was free of the clouds.

"Nice!"

She followed the path to the end, reaching the peak.

"That seemed more on the easy side."

She'd barely encountered any monsters, and it hadn't been that long since she entered.

She'd cleared dungeons very similar to this on lower floors, mostly for the materials they offered.

When she looked down, she found a small-petaled white flower growing by her feet.

The moment she touched it...

A sphere as white as the clouds fell from the flower.

Sally picked that up, checking the item name.

"Bubbles to Heaven?"

Since it was relatively easy to get another, Sally used it on the spot.

The sphere popped. Then bubbles, each a yard across, began rising up all around her, drifting into the sky above.

"Can I catch them?" she wondered.

When she reached out and touched one, it only yielded for a moment before bursting.

"Guess I just watch the show...it *is* pretty."

The bubbles were catching the light, glittering entrancingly underneath the sun's rays.

After a minute, they stopped generating, and the remaining bubbles drifted out of sight.

Part of Sally wished she'd found something more useful, but that was just how it went sometimes.

"Given how easy this place was, maybe that's appropriate. But I bet I end up coming here at least a few times for Maple's sake."

This was the kind of thing that always delighted her friend. She'd have to show Maple later.

Finding things that would tickle Maple's fancy was always high on her priority list.

Plus, this wasn't far from town and had only a few easy enemies, so it was no sweat at all.

"Right, let's find something else."

Sally headed back down the path out of the cumulonimbus dungeon.

◆□◆□◆□◆□◆

While Sally was out searching, Chrome and Kasumi were exploring on the opposite side of the map.

Chrome tanked the blows while Kasumi cut their foes down.

Sometimes he took damage, but his innate healing abilities quickly fixed that.

After the umpteenth successful fight, Chrome sheathed his weapon, muttering, "It's kinda relaxing."

"Mm? Ah yes..."

Out of all Maple Tree's members, these two had the most subdued fighting styles.

When Iz was around, the explosions never stopped.

With Kanade, spells were constantly roaring and flashing.

And the remaining four had a distinct tendency to rattle everyone watching them fight.

But right here, they were at peace.

"But taking down a dungeon boss with just the two of us is a tall order. I figure we're mostly just here to scout out any dungeons we find?"

"That sounds about right. If things get too tough, we can always call in for help."

Iz was generally an exception, but adding anyone else to their party would make a big difference.

"Sally's out exploring, too, so she should bring back good intel."

"Always does. We can decide how to proceed then."

As they walked, they heard the rumble of thunder. Ahead of them, dark clouds loomed.

Both drew their weapons, proceeding with caution, eyes on their surroundings.

As they drew closer, the landscape ahead came into view.

Clouds blotted out all traces of blue above, and bolts of electricity darted erratically between earth and sky.

Lightning strikes were making landfall every which way.

It was unclear if there was any pattern or how much damage it would do if any of them hit.

"Hmm. This calls for Maple," Chrome said.

"Let's turn back. We're not getting any farther."

Unwilling to risk that rain of lightning, they both turned and walked away.

Away from the high-voltage zone, Chrome and Kasumi went up and down the undulating clouds until they reached another cloudy area—albeit a slightly lighter shade of gray.

These clouds hung so low, it felt like you could reach out and touch them. And the terrain itself was so uneven that it was virtually impossible to see what lay ahead.

From these clouds fell softball-sized drops—and rather slowly, at that.

The precipitation was so floaty, it seemed almost weightless, but it clearly still headed steadily downward. Wherever the drops landed, they leisurely came apart, dividing into eight identical drops, each of which went its own way, ending its short journey after being absorbed into the ground.

"Think we should avoid those?"

"Probably a good idea."

They were relatively avoidable, but there were quite a lot of them, so it seemed best to find out the downside early.

"I'll go. If they do damage, I'm more likely to survive it."

He raised his shield and took a step forward, letting a drop hit him.

As it did, there was a sloshing sound behind him. Water was taking the shape of a cannon.

"Chrome! Behind you!"

"Mm? I can't…wha—?!"

He tried to move, but he was suddenly going even slower than the drops.

The cannon took a while to complete, but it was in his blind spot, and it wasn't clear if he would make it in time.

As he struggled, another drop landed near Chrome, and one of the smaller drops touched his leg.

And another cannon started forming diagonally behind him.

Chrome saw that mid-turn, and if he had been able to move freely, he definitely would have slapped a palm to his face and turned his gaze to the heavens above.

"Seriously?"

A blob of water shot out of the cannon, striking his shoulder— then the cannon itself collapsed.

The actual damage was probably 20 percent less than a normal hit from the average monsters on this stratum. Not particularly worrying on its own.

"Oh! I can move now!"

He twisted and rolled freely, finally escaping the rainy area.

Once he crossed the threshold, the second cannon collapsed without firing.

"Once a shell hits, you're back to normal speed, but every drop that touches you creates another cannon, huh?"

"You really couldn't move?"

"Yeah, that was definitely bad news. You can't just force your way through. Another hit is bound to come."

"Then we probably shouldn't push our luck. Want to head back into town?" Kasumi suggested. "There might be something there that helps clear the lightning or the slow rain."

Chrome nodded, and they abandoned their exploration efforts, opting to return to civilization.

*　　*　　*

They quickly dispatched all the monsters they came across and made steady progress until the sunlight vanished, and the world grew dim. As dusk arrived, the two of them finally stopped and looked up.

"That's…no ordinary cloud."

"I highly doubt it, yeah."

A very noticeable cloud was zooming over the field.

It felt just like the two areas they'd turned away from.

This cloud was *significant*.

And on this stratum, anything like that must mean something.

"How do we get up there?"

"Syrup?"

"I have a hunch that might lead us into some trouble. It *is* kinda cheating…"

It didn't seem like standing there thinking about it would get them anywhere, so they resumed their journey back to town.

◆□◆□◆□◆□◆

When Chrome and Kasumi made it back to the Guild Home, only Maple was around.

She was not feeling up to doing any exploring, so bringing her along was swiftly ruled out.

"Sally's out there somewhere, but…"

"And the other four aren't playing. All right, guess we'll have to try another day."

Chrome filled Maple in on everything they'd found.

"…I'll have to check those out."

Maple had her hand to her mouth, thinking. Neither of them could tell what was on her mind.

It might be nothing at all. It might also be something entirely unexpected.

Chrome and Kasumi both elected to say nothing more. Instead, they waved to her and disappeared into the back of the Guild Home.

"I wonder what Sally's doing..."

Maple leaned back in her chair, staring at the ceiling. That was when a message from the admins popped up.

She read it over. It was a brief description of the sixth event, coming in February.

"Jungle exploration, huh? Ugh, sounds like more rough footing."

Maple closed the message and got up, heading for her room.

"I guess I'll take it easy till then," she muttered.

Then she stopped in her tracks once before deciding to rest.

◆□◆□◆□◆□◆

Sally had continued exploring after clearing the cumulonimbus dungeon, racing around the map far longer than Chrome and Kasumi had. Now she was finally taking a break, leaning against some clouds by the side of the road.

"More like cumulonumerous..."

The farther she went, the more clouds she found with doors in them.

She'd checked a bunch out, hoping to find something special... and wound up with eight of the same thing in her inventory.

"Definitely don't need any more bubbles for a while..."

Sally was starting to think she'd picked the wrong side of the map. She got up, planning to head for new horizons...then thought better of it.

"Should I just call it for the day? Hmm…"

Exploring a cumulonimbus was a little like climbing a mountain.

The later ones had been smaller than the first, but not exactly relaxing.

Compared to the strain of the guild war during the fourth event, she was nowhere near her limit, but there was also no urgent need to rush things. Again, she considered just wrapping up her current session.

As she turned toward town, she looked up. Above her was a *real* cumulonimbus.

Sailing over her head.

"Whoa, what *is* that?"

Sally's eyes followed the cloud—she was impressed—and then she noticed something glitter in the distant sky.

"Is that…? Right, Superspeed!"

She raced past the cloud, getting ahead of it.

And the view from her new vantage point proved she'd been right.

Sally was right under the glittering spot.

And all around her, glistening soap bubbles were rising upward.

"There's gotta be *something* there…"

She raced around the cloud dungeon area again. The change was clear, but she couldn't figure out what the significance was.

"If that cloud gets here, it's time up! C'mon, gimme a clue!"

But the main cumulonimbus caught up with her, and she figured the jig was up.

"Oh, well…eeeep?!"

Just as she looked down, something gushed out from beneath her feet, flinging her upward.

"Oh? Whoa?! Um?"

Her body spun and spun, and when it finally stopped, all she could do was nervously look around. All this time in the game and nothing this freaky had ever happened to her.

She was currently on top of the cloud. She could hear the whistling wind, and there were bubbles filling the air. She slapped her cheeks and took a deep breath, calming her nerves.

"Okay, let's sort this out…"

She realized now that the gushing thing had been a stream of soap bubbles.

She'd been caught up in that on the ground and sent skyward.

"Focus…stay calm. Take your time."

There was a path—and so she followed it.

While scrutinizing the walls and floors, Sally moved down a narrow hall to a T junction.

Back up against the wall, she leaned slightly out, checking in both directions.

"!"

On the left, toward the end of the hall, she saw small glowing things hanging in the air. She ducked back behind cover before she had time to think.

Then a gust of wind roared down the cross-corridor.

The wind itself and the roar that came with it obscured things, but Sally's eyes caught softly glowing pale spheres flying within.

"…Hail?"

Whatever they were, they were clearly solid.

And they were hurtling down the hall like bullets. With her low HP and defense, any one of them could instantly kill Sally.

"Oookay, let's go right, then."

She decided it was in her best interests to *not* follow the wind. She jumped out into the hall.

"Ice Pillar!"

The ceilings here weren't that high, and her skill easily filled the space, blocking off a good chunk of the hall.

For another moment, the wind howled, hailstones rocketing past on one side of the barrier.

Then it went quiet.

"All done?" she muttered before peeling herself off the pillar and moving quickly down the hall.

She wasn't sure when or if a second wave would hit, so her eye never left the corridor behind her.

"Ah, figured it was a bust."

Everything was white and rounded, making it hard to tell if there was a turn up ahead or not. This forced her to inspect every dead end up close.

Even when the hall abruptly ended, she only had to work her way backward, so it wasn't a serious problem.

And this way, she could be certain there was nothing behind her.

She moved along, ready to act if the wind blew again—but her fears proved unfounded.

It seemed the wind was a trap that only activated when you first entered.

Sally reached the far end of the other passage and found a new path leading upward.

At the top of that was a large room with nothing remarkable inside it.

Besides the three passages leading out, of course.

"Cross this... Guess I'll start on the right."

But as she reached the center of the room, blue-tinted cloud monsters spawned from the floor and ceiling.

There were ten of them in all, each wreathed in some sort of white mist.

"Fire Ball!"

Given the close brush with hail, she'd figured this white mist was aligned with the ice element, so she quickly hit one with a fire spell.

The flames certainly dropped the HP bar hard, but it still had a solid 60 percent left.

"That's all I get even when I'm using something they're weak against?"

These days, players without much MP reserves—like Sally—were struggling to make much headway with spells.

An instant later, she sensed the wind at her back and immediately took evasive maneuvers.

"These monsters *also* use hail..."

In Sally's mind, the hail here and in the hall was like a focused beam attack. Tracking her position versus the ten clouds, she took the fight back.

"Oboro, Fleeting Shadow!"

For a moment, she was free of aggro. Drawing her daggers, she closed in on the cloud she'd burned.

"Double Slash!"

Sword Dance had boosted her attack quite high.

The stream of combos she dished out scattered cloud after cloud, each melting into the air.

"Sweet! Clouds are a cakewalk!"

Sally chewed through the crowd like a silent dance, like a well-rehearsed routine.

No wasted motions. She only traveled the shortest path to robbing them of HP.

Even with their hail attacks, they never even scratched her.

"Whew, thanks, Oboro! Now for that path on the right..."

She gave her fox a rub and resumed her exploration. It didn't take her long after that encounter to learn that this cloud was like an ant nest.

Passages often branched up, down, left, and right. Many of the passages had hail or ice spike traps, impeding her progress.

The bigger rooms were home not just to little clouds, but also ice golems and wind monsters.

Sally's fire spells weren't that great, and monsters made of ice were surprisingly tanky, so they were painful to fight, but since none of them could lay an icicle on her, she eventually wore them all down.

Their advantages did not ensure victory.

Sally weathered another storm of hail, checked that she was safe for the moment, and then rapidly slumped to the ground.

"I've gotta be pretty high up...," she said, stroking Oboro's fur.

She glanced at the hall ahead. The enemies in this cloud weren't really a problem for her, but the layout and all these traps were both wearing her out.

"Let's hope the goal's close. Come on, Oboro."

The path she followed was growing narrower, and the forks became fewer in number.

Finally, she spotted a color other than white.

There was a wall ahead with a blue magic circle on it that glowed softly.

Something was waiting on the other side, no doubt.

"Mm, I'm ready."

She reached out and touched the circle.

There was a *crackle*, and she was transported away.

*　　*　　*

The second she arrived, she drew both daggers and spun around, searching for danger.

She was in a dome made of thick clouds, like standing underneath an overcast sky.

The ground at her feet and the dome itself were made of the same materials as the dungeon she'd just been exploring.

"...There!"

Not missing the faintest sound, Sally swung at it.

Slipping between the clouds beneath her was an arm made of ice. Like any bona fide monster, it had an HP bar above it.

Incidentally, it was also three times her height and started at the elbow. It grew straight up from the clouds, but the moment it noticed her, it sank back in—reappearing right before her eyes.

The arm formed a fist before swinging it down at Sally like a hammer.

"Ha!"

Sally saw it coming, of course, and slipped right past it to run directly to the base of the arm.

She slashed at the side in passing like she was keying a car, but it did less than she was expecting; this thing must have had *high* defense.

Worse, she hadn't foreseen its counter.

As the monster's fist struck the ground, a ripple spread out from the impact.

Sally was well within range, and it forced her to break stride.

Then the frozen vapor hanging around the arm grew much thicker.

It was clearly readying an attack.

"! Okay, Leap!"

She recovered her footing in the nick of time, allowing her to put as much distance between her and the arm as she could.

As if giving chase, ice thorns shot out of the floor around the arm, covering the ground of the dome—but Sally managed to stay one step ahead and avoid getting hit.

Soon after, the ice thorns crumbled and melted away.

"If I don't have both Leap and Superspeed ready, I can't risk countering that attack."

Carefully running down her mental checklist, she was forced to jump away without offering any retaliation the next time the arm came in close and swung at her.

"Fire Ball!"

She swung back as she fled, flinging a spell.

It landed on the wrist. Not much damage to speak of, but every bit mattered here.

"Let's see where that gets me."

Sally didn't mind long battles. And this fight was one-on-one, the kind of fight she was best at.

She'd decided to play it safe by beating this thing slow and steady.

Fire worked well on ice.

Even the weakest spell did visible damage, which was not bad at all.

Half an hour later, she had the monster down to 60 percent health.

"*Sigh...*"

Sally glared at the ice arm, looking frustrated.

It had made two clouds, both of which were throwing hail around.

She'd gotten good at dodging those and wasn't exactly struggling, but it was still utterly annoying.

She focused her concentration again as she began to make another approach.

Monsters had no emotions, but if this one did, it would have been afraid of her by now. She dodged *everything*.

No matter how furiously it attacked, nothing hit Sally.

With Ice Pillar to give her hiding spots on demand, it would need a lot more projectiles and much higher attack speed.

When the arm's HP hit 40 percent, four more clouds appeared. There were now six in total.

"I'm still in this...whoa!"

A magic circle had suddenly appeared beneath her feet, forcing her to jump away.

She hadn't moved a moment too soon, as a needlelike icicle shot up from it just as she cleared the space.

It did nothing else and quickly crumbled away.

She looked up and saw the arm holding its palm to the ceiling, apparently summoning more blue magic circles.

Some were already deploying by Sally's feet, giving chase. She could no longer afford to stand still. Hiding behind her Ice Pillar wouldn't cut it anymore.

"......"

Could she run headlong into this barrage and make it through?

This thought wasn't motivated directly by this battle, but it did provide the final push to make her try.

"If I take damage...well, fine. I wanna try."

Sally used Doping Seeds to boost her STR as high as she could get it, then dashed directly toward the ice arm.

Nimbly dodging the hail or batting it aside with her daggers, she was practically on top of her target in no time.

"Hah!"

She swung both blades, stabbing the arm.

The HP bar lurched, dropping far beyond what most people would have thought possible with just daggers.

She started circle strafing it, following up with more blows. Once it reached 10 percent health, the ground around it glowed blue.

She kept raining attacks on the arm, and sharp ice stabbed her before the arm went down.

But Shed Skin kicked in, and she took no damage.

And her all-out attack finished off the HP bar before the arm could attack again.

The battle ended with the *ding* of a system message.

She stretched.

"Not half bad," she said, nodding to herself.

And checked the message.

She'd gained a new skill.

"Subzero Domain?"

Subzero Domain

Usable for ten minutes after using any water-based skill.
Freezes magic or objects.
No direct impact on players or monsters.
Applies the ice element to all attacks, friend or foe.

"Fair enough. Plus, it seems like anyone who beats that thing can get it, after all... Seems like a good place to wrap up."

She put her daggers away. The arm's demise had generated an exit circle, so she took that out of the cloud.

CHAPTER 9

Defense Build and a Comeback

Some time had passed since Sally gained her new skill. It was February, and the sixth event was fast approaching.

Sally, Chrome, and Kasumi—the gamer group—were all ready to dive in.

Maple was back from a long break, finally motivated to explore again. She logged in soon after the event began.

As Maple reached the Guild Home, Chrome and Kasumi were flying out the door.

She turned and watched them go. Sally came up behind her and patted her shoulder.

"Glad to see you're back. Gonna explore today?"

"Yep! Finally felt up to it."

"Then lemme give you a quick rundown on the event. Like the second one, this one's exploration-based. The goal is to find some stuff and make it home in one piece."

She proceeded to fill Maple in on the finer details.

The first thing players had to do was hit up the regular field, searching for an item that looked like a green crystal. Using those would transport them to the event map. But *where* the crystal took them was completely random.

There were no PVP elements or time dilation.

"Also, the event map is a jungle. Most rewards are gonna be valuable materials. Maaaybe some skills?"

"Cool, cool."

"Oh, and the clincher—while you're in the jungle, you can't rely on HP recovery items or skills. In your case…Meditation is outright unusable."

Anyone who died or hit the LEAVE MAP button on their stat menu would be immediately sent back to town.

"So I'd better not use Martyr's Devotion lightly?"

Sally nodded.

Using any skills that cost HP was a big risk.

But since Maple rarely had to worry about attacks in the first place, she had a big advantage over other players.

"Anyway, I'm gonna go look for a crystal myself," Sally said, one foot already out the door.

"Have fun!"

Maple headed to the field as well, moving at her own pace.

◆☐◆☐◆☐◆☐◆

"Okay, let's look this over again…"

Sally had explained the gist, and Maple had a solid idea what she was doing.

There were no specific monsters that had to be defeated. Jungle tickets could drop from any monster on the stratum.

This was Maple's first time properly exploring the fifth stratum, and she decided to do just that while hunting monsters along the way.

She stepped out on the springy ground, keeping her head on swivel.

"Sally said there were lots of cloud monsters..."

Maple clambered over a cloud wall before heading down the hill. The terrain sure was *rolling*.

"But I don't see *any* enemies. Should I head back down a floor?"

She considered it but then spotted a cumulonimbus up ahead, which gave her an idea.

These specific clouds had come up in tales of Sally's exploits. There was a good chance she would find monsters inside.

And Maple had already used up the bubble items Sally had given her, so she figured she could also get a new one while she was at it.

"All right, I'm going— Yikes?! Aughhh!"

Maple slipped and went rolling all the way down the hill.

"Ugh...at least it doesn't hurt. But I'd better be careful."

She got back up and started picking her way forward.

Right inside the cumulonimbus entrance, Maple found a thunderhead.

"I haven't fought in so long!"

She sprouted artillery and aimed it all at the little cloud.

But before she could attack, the crackling cloud started splitting off mini monster clouds.

"...So cute!"

Forgetting all about attacking, she reached out to pet the little clouds, which tried to electrocute her, but it only made a bunch of *zaaap* sounds. Nothing else happened.

"I really do have to get one of these items. Sorry!"

She stepped up to the main cloud and tapped her shield to it.

"Aaaand...no drops."

Ultimately, Maple failed to get the event access item.

All she earned for her troubles was another bubble item.

But Maple had fun exploring, so whatever the results, she didn't mind.

Maple didn't get a jungle access item until two days later.

Not exactly first in line, but she'd found one with plenty of time left in the event, so she picked a day when she could play for a while and decided to scope out the event map until then.

"Okay! It's time! Crystal, go!"

She held up the item and was wreathed in light.

The beam shot toward the heavens and left without a trace.

When the light cleared, she found herself in a quiet jungle. The only sound was the rustling of leaves in the wind.

Trees towered overhead, vines dangling between them.

"Well…not much around me."

She detected no players or monsters.

The event map spawns were totally random.

Sally, Chrome, and Kasumi were probably here somewhere, but finding them would be a tall order.

"I wanna find at least one good item or skill. That would make the trip worth it!"

Maple enthusiastically set out into the jungle.

She looked right and left, searching for anything out of the ordinary. Then she spied a pretty red flower.

It had five big petals, each as long as her arm, and gave off a sweet scent.

"Wonder if that's something?"

She moved closer to investigate.

As if it had been waiting for that, the flower's stem extended, and the petals wrapped around Maple's upper body.

And they knocked her sword and shield aside, forcing her to drop them both.

Objectively speaking, it absolutely looked like she was being eaten.

"Wha—?! S-stop that!"

Maple was thrashing her arms and legs, more out of reflex than conscious choice.

The flower refused to let go.

But it also wasn't doing any damage.

"Oh, right!"

Recovering from the shock, she remembered that she had a way to attack without equipment. She deployed a bunch of guns.

The flower was wholly focused on eating Maple and never realized what peril it was in.

"Commence Assault!"

Bullet after bullet tore the flower to shreds, eventually freeing Maple.

"Wow, that was a rough surprise!"

She picked up her sword and shield...but the fight wasn't over yet.

Just before the flower monster vanished, it sprayed something sweet into the air.

As the fragrance spread outward, it soon became clear this was no aromatherapy.

"Wh-what now?"

She could hear the brush swaying, leaves rustling, and something heavy thudding toward her. The jungle was quiet no longer.

The noises grew louder, quickly surrounding Maple. Birds,

monkeys, moving plants, and even a giant made of moss-covered boulders all appeared at the same time.

"Uh-oh...," Maple said, making a face. The horde was only ten yards out and closing in.

Even Maple could easily surmise the flower's scent had drawn them here.

The noble sacrifices of players before her probably meant everyone else was already well aware that the flowers' death throes summoned a mob, but since Sally was basically Maple's only source of information, she'd had no clue.

But unlike her predecessors, Maple was not so easily martyred.

"Kinda hard to fly away in a jungle...so I guess I *gotta* fight!"

Maple wasn't particularly fanatical about standing her ground, but nevertheless, she was perfectly capable of doing so when push came to shove. She deployed all her weapons, ready for combat.

"Commence Assault!"

Not even attempting to aim at any monster in particular, Maple just sprayed the area with cannon shells and lasers, devastating her surroundings.

The trees blocked a lot of it, and her artillery couldn't unleash its full potential, but that was more than enough for the weaker monsters.

Unfortunately, there were some more agile foes using the trees as cover to slip past her initial bombardment.

"Predators!"

A pair of monsters lurched up from the ground on either side of her, letting nothing get close.

Maple was just too tanky. Unable to realize the futility of their assault, the monsters kept coming, only to be rent asunder.

"Any damage? Nope, nope! I'm all good!"

She kept a close eye on the stone giant in case it did anything noteworthy, backing steadily away even as she attacked it.

Her summons handled anything that tried approaching her from behind, so she didn't ever need to look back.

The sounds of death and destruction coming from that direction made that perfectly clear.

"Okay, if I keep this up…"

Some bird monsters above were using ranged attacks, but those simply bounced off her. The ground was more or less clear of enemies.

Things were going well, and she started to relax.

"Guess it was nothing to worr—mm?!"

She'd just seen a red flower pop out from under the giant's feet.

Maple quickly halted her attack but was a second too slow—a laser struck the flower's stamen.

"Nooo!"

The same sweet fragrance from before filled the air, and the noisy jungle became even noisier.

"Why was that there?! Aaaargh!" she wailed, waving both arms up and down.

◆□◆□◆□◆□◆

The formerly quiet jungle was now filled with the riotous sounds of combat.

More players were spawning—and Pain was one of them.

"Ha!"

He bashed a monster with his shield and finished it with his blade.

Pain had been surrounded, but he made short work of his foes.

"All done. Let's see what I got for my trouble."

He checked the items the monsters had dropped but found nothing worth writing home about.

Pain had already found several moss-covered ruins but hadn't unearthed anything valuable from any of them.

"I should be more careful."

His HP was already down 30 percent.

He hadn't suffered any serious direct damage, but the sheer number of monsters had steadily chipped away at his health reserves.

And since recovery was impossible, he had to avoid damage wherever he could.

Pain set out once more, hoping to find something new.

As he walked, his ears picked up the faint sounds of battle in the distance. He'd been in this jungle a while but had rarely heard fighting this close by.

He'd been making full use of the intel he'd gathered and avoided challenging foes or circumventing picked-over areas. Even so, he still had yet to find a new skill.

"I wouldn't mind seeing if they're onto something."

Pain drew near the battle, but the underbrush was too high, and he couldn't get a good look.

But his instincts were telling him this was no ordinary fight.

He'd never seen foliage this thick, and that alone was enough to arouse his suspicions. If he simply bypassed this, he might miss out on valuable items or skills. With that in mind, he drew his sword, pushing forward with caution.

"...Let's see what lies within."

Just as Pain parted the last of the brush, the noises up ahead stopped.

There was a rustling that marked something's passage—something that was headed right toward him.

Pain braced his shield and stepped out of the brush, ready to fight whoever was coming his way. The sound grew louder and louder until finally, a hideous face loomed overhead.

"Ah-ha!"

Pain looked up and saw the visage of a monster. One he would not soon forget.

"I'm so tired…oh, hey! You're Pain, right?"

The monster's face had no eyes.

But Pain had heard this voice before.

Maple's voice was quite distinctive, after all.

They moved a short distance away, settling down in a clearing. Maple was still in monster form.

Since recovery was limited, she didn't want to release Atrocity until she had to.

Pain sat down on a tree root, and Maple leaned her long body against the tree itself.

"You're…just gonna stay like that?"

"……? Um, yes."

"Okay then…"

Pain was a tad unsettled by it, but he assumed she had limited uses, so he didn't argue the point. Besides, he was well aware of just how powerful this form was.

They were together for a reason—they'd decided to explore that way.

Two top players had happened across each other on a field so vast, it was more likely to encounter no one at all. Maple might not have realized the significance of that, but Pain hadn't failed to notice. And it was a prime opportunity to observe anything new she had up her sleeve.

He'd been the one to propose they team up, and Maple had no objections.

She hadn't spared the suggestion much thought. To her mind, playing with someone strong was always a good thing, and Pain seemed like he could be relied upon.

And thus the most powerful duo in the game's history was born.

"Luck is with us. This should speed up our explorations."

"Totally! I can handle all the defense!"

Maple and Pain continued pushing deeper into the jungle.

"Maple…"

"What's up?"

"Uh…never mind. I was just thinking…you're really good at handling yourself in that form."

"I don't really get why, though! I just can!"

"Huh…," Pain said, his eyes turning upward.

The green canopy hid the sky from view, flowing by as he remained immobile.

In other words, he was sitting on monster Maple's back.

She was threading her way through the trunks, definitely feeling a little constricted.

"Maple, turn left. There was nothing to the right."

"Got it!"

Maple lurched sideways. If any other players saw them, they'd almost certainly ready themselves for imminent combat.

Or possibly cling to a nearby tree trunk. Maybe even race off through the trees with their tails between their legs.

Pain found it pretty easy to stay put on her back, so a few sudden moves on her part wouldn't be enough to shake him off.

There was nothing impeding their search.

"Oh, monsters! I'll just kill them."

There were, indeed, foes up ahead.

"That's a treant. Careful, Maple," Pain warned. For good reason—these were the enemies that had managed to damage him. "They've got a piercing attack that comes from below."

"Mm? What was that?"

Before he could finish, Maple had turned the area in front of them into a sea of fire.

The inferno didn't spread out, but they were definitely not the kind of wimpy flames anything made of wood could easily withstand.

The treants turned to ash and yielded their items.

"Never mind," Pain said. "You should pick those up."

"Good call!"

Maple used her monster hands to collect the items and tuck them into her inventory.

Seeing her steamroll all these enemies without a care in the world drove home once more the gap between her and everyone else.

They were attacked several times on the way, but Maple simply trampled the monsters underfoot or otherwise knocked them away.

"......Did you just run over something else?"

"They just keep attacking!"

"I feel like you're the one—actually, forget it. Just watch out for trees. They're tougher than the monsters."

He watched her flatten yet another foe. This was definitely not your typical field expedition. But since she was handling all the combat and movement, he was left free to focus on other things.

"Maple, stop. I hear something."

He'd only noticed because he was free to scan their surroundings.

And his ears had caught the sound of buzzing wings.

"Should we go take a look?"

"Let's."

Maple wasn't really built for stealth, but she *felt* like she was sneaking. As they neared the buzzing, they saw a bee's nest at the top of a tree.

And a black stripe surrounding it.

Since the buzzing was coming from that stripe, they could guess why it was undulating.

"Interesting. Thoughts?"

"I could draw them away and keep you safe?"

"Will it really be that easy? Well, I guess it would be."

Pain had started considering the idea's pros and cons, then realized there was no point.

Since there was an HP restriction in effect, and Pain was good at gaming, Maple decided she didn't need to baby him and left Martyr's Devotion inactive.

"Let's do this!"

Maple jumped out into the clearing under the bee's nest. Up near it was a bee—one nearly four yards long.

It had a beautiful crown on its head.

It was literally a queen bee.

"That looks stronger than the first bee I fought!" Maple observed aloud.

The queen bee buzzed.

In response, the black bee belt above turned as one, immediately launching themselves at Maple like a torrent of arrows.

They hit her hard and proceeded to bounce right off.

"Taunt! Keep coming!"

The queen bee continued buzzing orders. It tried focused attacks, encircling Maple and hitting her in the flanks, but all the bees bounced away, dizzily awaiting the next order.

"...Holy Rain."

In the shadow of a tree, Pain drew his sword, whispering. The blade began to glow.

A swing of his blade sent the built-up energy surging forward.

It stopped ten yards away—right above the clearing where Maple was fighting. Then it began to rain streaks of light down upon the battlefield.

The bees were too focused on Maple to realize the light was killing them.

While Maple was frolicking with the bees, Pain became a machine, using all the AOEs he had.

"What am I even doing...?"

"Keep chewing through them like this!"

"...All right! Leave it to me!"

He spied a bee breaking its stinger on her monster hide.

If you ignored...a lot of things, this was...an effective approach. Really, it was all upsides.

It was just... The visuals were far removed from what most people saw on a day-to-day basis.

It took about twenty minutes to dispatch all the bees. Once that was done, Pain finally joined Maple in the clearing.

"Uninjured? Naturally."

"Pain, the queen bee's coming!"

He looked up.

She was right—it was slowly descending toward them.

"I'll finish it in one."

Pain cast stray thoughts—and Maple—out of his mind and raised his sword.

"Yeah, let's do this!"

Maple raised her head.

Courageous or foolhardy, the queen bee was descending into the jaws of death.

When the bee reached the halfway point between the nest and its foes, the hives themselves came loose, falling away from the tree.

The queen nimbly avoided them, and the fragments hurtled directly toward Maple and Pain.

"Cover Move! Cover!"

This was one of the few combos Maple had managed to memorize. She placed herself directly over Pain.

The fallen hives splattered, coating them with the honey inside.

"Uh...I—I can't move!"

Sticky honey had Maple completely immobilized. If Maple had met a certain STR threshold, that would have posed no problem, but since her base Strength was zero, even in Atrocity form, her stats didn't reach very high.

The queen bee charged at the sticky Maple, trying its hardest to get that stinger in, or maybe bite her.

The attack patterns weren't particularly complicated—the queen was still at full health—and the only trick it seemed to have was a wind spell.

But naturally, none of those did anything to Maple, so it was all as futile as it was industrious.

"Guess it's up to me."

Pain emerged from beneath Maple's bulk, approaching the queen from behind.

That was enough to draw the queen bee's aggro, and it fired a poison needle at him.

But he easily deflected it with his shield and took a swing before it recovered from the attack motion.

"Holy Condemnation!"

The horizontal sword stroke sent his gleaming blade right into the queen bee's torso.

Pain's attack carried all the force he'd once used against Maple herself.

No miraculous salvation was there to protect the queen, so the fatal blow cut it clean in half. It quickly turned into particles of light.

And all the honey imprisoning Maple vanished with it.

Once the boss was gone, it left behind a number of honey bottles and two crowns.

Pain examined both of these.

Honey Jar

Ingredient found only in the jungle area.
Increases maximum HP by 50 for two minutes. Does not stack.

Queen Bee's Crown

When equipped, increases equipped player's maximum MP and MP recovery speed by 10% each.

They split the drops evenly before setting out again.

That small a boost in MP wouldn't grant Maple an extra use of Hydra or her other big spells. She knew the crown would not be immediately useful, but it was pretty, so she was happy with it.

"Wanna try going that way?" she suggested, indicating a direction with one of her many limbs.

"Why not? This jungle's huge. There's bound to be something good out there."

"Then come on!"

Maple let Pain climb aboard again and began threading her way through the trees once more.

CHAPTER 10

Defense Build and the Web Spinner

There was Maple, and there was Pain.

But of course—they weren't the only ones out there.

Specifically, Sally was also deep in the jungle. Quite a distance lay between her and Maple, but Sally didn't know that.

This was a field devoid of obvious landmarks, making it impossible to meet up with anyone by design, so it didn't really matter who else might be playing.

And so Sally was darting through the jungle with speed.

"Anything heeere?"

She vaulted over a fallen tree and was about to keep running, but then something caught her eye, and she drew up short.

"Hmm? Is that...?"

She narrowed her eyes, peering into the distance.

Something in all that green seemed out of place, but at this range, she couldn't tell what.

"Guess I'd better get closer."

She drew her daggers and pushed her way through the rustling underbrush.

Proximity improved her view.

"Yeesh, a spiderweb. I'm not great at fighting things that fling sticky crap around..."

She made a face but kept going. She was *that* hungry for skills.

"If the tide turns against me, I can always run. Anyway, let's see what we've got here."

Sally stopped near the web, scanning the area.

Webs of thread ran between several different trees and across the ground itself. No sign of any spiders.

But she did see some white cocoons near the ground.

"That looks like a trap...but if I'm quick, I oughtta be able to check that."

Her mind made up, Sally nodded to herself.

"Superspeed!"

She darted out from behind the tree and tapped one of the cocoons.

"Items? Skills? Nope! Argh..."

Unsurprisingly, it *was* a trap. She had figured as much.

What she hadn't counted on was how large an area it affected. The thread on the ground around her covered such a large area that even with Superspeed, she couldn't dodge it in time.

That was how Sally found herself hanging upside down, thread snarled around one foot.

"I swear one of these got me before...that's why I hate them! Dammit."

A large spider scuttled into view.

"Argh, crap, crap!"

She put her abs to work, making herself swing.

The thread on her foot was *not* coming off, but she wasn't completely snared yet so it wasn't all bad news.

"Better than I'd feared..."

That said, she'd still have to do whatever she could and try to stave off sudden death.

The spider didn't give her time to plan.

It scurried up a web-wrapped trunk and was right on top of her in no time at all.

This had happened to her in another game, and the result had been an untimely death.

"I could...or...argh, I can't think straight! Ice Pillar!"

The spider had made it close enough that one ice spike after another plowed into it.

"Not expecting much damage, but...there we go!"

Sally saw the spider change its pathing, grabbing onto one of the pillars to hang on.

From there, it could not directly attack Sally—but since it was bigger than her, it made for a perfect target.

"Fire Ball! Wind Cutter!"

Her spells were relatively feeble, but they were definitely doing damage.

"Mirage!"

Sally cast an illusion of herself, and the spider took the bait.

Certain it was heading away, Sally made an attempt at cutting the thread with magic.

It remained impervious.

She glanced over at the HP bar hovering above the spider.

Still at 85 percent.

"...I'll have to one-shot it when it comes close again."

The damage she'd done so far proved she didn't have enough MP to down it with ranged spells. Once it was back in effective range, she'd have to finish it off so fast that it wouldn't even have a chance to hit her.

"Time for some Doping Seeds? I can still null one hit—so I'm not ready to give up yet."

It slew the fake Sally and then came back along the tree trunk toward her.

She took out a Doping Seed and popped it into her mouth.

This raised STR at a cost of VIT, boosting her DPS. She armed herself with her daggers, practiced her plan of attack a few times, then waited for the spider to get there.

The spider was directly above her now. It started climbing down the thread attached to her leg.

"Double Slash!"

She used the backswing to right herself, her daggers striking the spider's face and legs just before its fangs sank into her knee.

But these attacks were from such a precarious position that several of them missed. The spider still had a solid 20 percent HP.

And it didn't let her assault go unpunished.

The spider's entire body flashed, and thread came flying out.

For a moment, it hovered near the spider, but then it rocketed toward Sally.

"Argh...!"

There was no way for her to dodge it properly. By guarding with her left side and throwing the right-hand dagger, she managed to keep her right hand free.

"Impact Fist!"

This was a skill that fired air bullets—one she'd used to propel Maple after the giant squid.

The attack hit the spider's face, and red sparks flew around its many little eyes.

It shot back even more thread, and that was when Sally realized something serious.

All her skills were sealed.

This applied to her gear as well—she couldn't even summon Oboro.

That wouldn't have mattered if she'd managed to down the spider—but it was still hanging on.

"Seriously? That didn't kill it?"

There were only a few dots left on its HP bar. One more hit would finish it.

It wound more webbing around her, moving toward her throat in preparation for the finisher.

"There's gotta be—"

As she racked her brains, the spider's mandibles scraped at Sally's neck.

Shed Skin activated, canceling this damage—but now she had no way of preventing whatever came next.

"......!"

She twisted herself, making the thread sway.

The spider's fangs closed in again.

But a moment later, red sparks flew—and its HP hit zero.

"Heh-heh...tough break, buddy!" Sally crowed.

She was laughing her head off.

And rolling a little eye around her mouth.

The spider began dissolving into light.

Just before the head changed, she thought its remaining eyes met hers through the shower of sparks.

"Blame Maple," she said.

And with a shattering sound, it was gone.

"Blegh, that's nasty!"

An emotionless voice echoed in her head.

The sound of a new skill.

◆□◆□◆□◆□◆

When the battle ended, the thread binding Sally began to vanish.

Once her upper body was free, she pulled her head up—

—and when the last of the thread vanished, she began to fall.

"Hokay…"

She managed to get her legs down in time and land upright.

"I know I got a skill… Yup, there it is!"

She had her stat menu open.

Web Spinner I had just been added.

She read the description.

Web Spinner I

Manipulate spiderwebs.
At skill level V, adds control of elasticity.
Five-yard range. Can be fired from both hands and legs.
Use again to release.

"So not an eater skill? Oh, but it has the same conditions."

When she was done reading, she decided to try the skill out.

"A test-drive seems in order. Web Spinner!"

Her stat screen was still up, and as she spoke, it changed.

The words *Web Spinner* appeared by her name.

She read the description again and this time held out her right hand.

"Right Hand: Web."

The same spider silk that had bound her a moment ago shot out of her right palm. It hit a tree ahead of her, binding it.

She put her back into it, tugging, but the thread wouldn't let go.

Sally thought about this one.

"...Maple, I'm gonna take a page from your book this time," she muttered.

She released the web, then headed deeper in, looking to raise the skill level.

Sally would have preferred to get on Maple's level by entirely different means.

But perhaps she was just being obstinate.

Firing and releasing webs, she moved through the jungle—then paused.

"I've at least gotta get it to level V and see what the elasticity does for it."

But she felt like it was too risky to level the skill here. She decided to leave the jungle for now.

This skill was more compelling than the event.

"Can't afford to die just yet. Time to go."

Her body soon turned to light, leaving the jungle behind.

Armed with her new skill, Sally arrived back at the fifth stratum Guild Home.

Inside, she found Kanade and Chrome.

She talked to them a bit and found they were both about to head into the jungle.

"I'm giving it another run," Chrome said. "Haven't found anything yet but materials for Iz."

"There's something I've got my eye on, but I'm not sure if I can make it there or not. Gotta try, though!" Kanade said.

Each of them had their own goals, and if they succeeded, the guild would be that much stronger for it.

"Have fun. And good luck."

"Yeah, I'll bring something back."

"Same here!"

They all waved and were soon out the door.

Around this time, two members of Flame Empire were headed to the jungle, too.

They started their exploration shortly before Chrome and Kanade.

Perhaps destiny played a hand in this development, but the Maple Tree members happened to spawn right in their paths.

That was how Kanade and Marx paired up, while Chrome ran into Misery.

Mages or any other MP-dependent classes were after only one thing—skills that buffed MP.

Both Kanade and Marx wanted those—and since their motives aligned, they readily agreed to work together.

Chrome similarly agreed to help Misery with the same thing.

And then Maple came charging through the jungle with Pain on her back.

"Oh," he said. "Supposedly, you can get an MP boost skill that way."

"Sounds good!" she said.

Pain was getting strangely used to riding monsters.

All three pairs independently converged on the MP buff skill location.

Then Chrome and Misery ran into a pack of monsters.

"Take that!" Chrome's cleaver struck a moss-covered golem.

Unlike Maple, he had a formidable attack and was able to hurt these things.

But the golem was not their only foe.

Wolves and monkeys were trying their best to flank him.

"Not on my watch!"

Misery's bolts of light blew several of them away.

And that gave Chrome time to get his shield in position.

This map's conditions blocked any and all healing, which left them both very underpowered.

This team composition would normally mean Misery's healing spells and Chrome's self-healing skills would make him an impregnable fortress, but that wasn't the case here in the jungle.

So they both had to proceed with a lot more caution.

"Holy, there's no end to them!"

"Let's make a run for it. I've got an escape item somewhere... here!"

She scanned through her inventory, pulled out a white ball, and tossed it at the ground.

Smoke filled the area, temporarily blinding the monsters.

That distraction allowed the two of them to make a clean getaway.

"Whew...there's a limit to how much I can tank alone."

"*Sigh*... Having an attacker with us would make it much easier for me."

"When the twins or Maple are around, I never have to think like this..."

"With Mii or Shin in my party, I know they'll handle everything."

Everyone they just named was among the game's most powerful players, but these two were handling combat perfectly fine, really. Neither of their classes was really built for exploration, so getting by despite their grumbling just proved they were *also* top players. And the farther they went, the more they learned, and the better their internal maps of the route to the heart of the jungle became.

◆□◆□◆□◆□◆

While they grimly hung in there, Kanade and Marx were battling their own group of monsters.

"Here they come…," Marx announced, never even breaking stride.

Kanade had his bookshelves out but wasn't reaching for any grimoires.

Just as the monsters were about to pounce, thick vines shot out of the ground, coiling around the monkeys and birds.

Above Marx's head, the monsters were flailing about, trying to free themselves to no avail.

"And now, detonate."

Red magic circles appeared around the vines, and the ensuing explosions hit all the monsters.

Marx's next spell polished off the stragglers.

"Oh, nicely done."

"Once they're snared, it's nothing."

Marx didn't exactly look excited, but there was a noticeable flicker of pride.

But then he spotted a moss-covered golem several times his size.

And its red eyes met his.

"Oh, nope. Nope on that one."

"Mm, then…well, I don't know where else I'd use this. Death's Call."

A slim black book slipped off Kanade's shelves.

The cover was speckled with blood. The pages flipped

automatically, and there was a low tone that seemed to echo in their guts.

The massive golem was then sheathed in bottomless darkness before exploding into countless motes of light.

"Oh, it worked. Low chance of instant death."

"You're lucky, then?"

"A little."

They started walking again.

Clearly having a much easier time than Chrome and Misery.

◆□◆□◆□◆□◆

Elsewhere, in the noisiest part of the jungle…

Tossing aside monsters in passing, or burning them, or trampling them underfoot. If anything tried to run, it was hit by glowing sword strokes.

This was how Maple stampeded through the dungeon, not caring if any monsters came her way, and Pain had come along for the ride.

"Oh? Maple, stop for a second. I saw something."

"Yeah? Okay!"

She took out one last foe as she skidded to a halt.

A fair distance from them, several trees were strangely misshapen, as if they'd been partially melted.

Both of them moved closer to inspect the scene.

The bent trees led them farther in. Eventually, they came upon an extra-large tree made by winding the trunks of several others together.

There was an opening at the base, containing a room with a staircase that led higher into the tree.

"Oh, is this…?"

"The place I told you about, yes."

Maple compared her monstrous bulk to the size of the door.

It didn't look like she would fit.

She was forced to come out of Atrocity mode.

The monster's belly split open, and Maple fell out with a *splat*.

Pain watched that happen, bemused, then went to confirm the entrance was safe.

"Not seeing anything wrong."

"Then I'll go first!"

Maple waved her shield emphatically, and Pain gave her a nod.

They started picking their way up the stairs.

They were on guard the whole way but reached the end without incident.

At the top, there was a bough so wide, it could easily accommodate both of them.

There was a gentle breeze, and the leaves rustled softly overhead. Soothing sights and sounds all around.

At the end of the branch was a green magic circle.

"We wanna go in, right?"

"That's why we're here."

Their footsteps ran down the length of the branch. As they came closer, the circle's glow grew brighter, seemingly inviting them in.

When Maple stepped on it, her body was wreathed in green light, and she vanished from view.

Pain followed shortly after, and they both found themselves somewhere else entirely.

Where the jungle had been filled with noise, this new forest was eerily silent.

Rows of trees. Green leaves.

Shrubs laden with glistening red fruit. The blue sky far above.

But not a single sound to make the forest feel alive. No birds singing, no leaves rustling—even their footsteps seemed silent.

"Are we...?"

Maple ventured to ask a question, making the first sound they'd heard since arriving.

"This is the source of the MP buff skill," Pain explained. Maple seemed lost, so he was reminding her of their goal. Pain wanted a higher MP recovery rate, and Maple was intrigued by the possibilities.

"Got it!" she said. "We've come all this way, so let's give it a shot!"

"Then we should get moving. This place requires us to follow the right path, so I'll take the lead."

Pain had done his homework and knew exactly which way to go. He checked their path against his intel and led them through the soundless woods.

"Don't leave my side. If you step off the prescribed route, monsters will spawn."

Maple stuck to him like glue.

They moved on. Pain began giving her the rundown on the boss.

She listened close, ready to tackle this fight effectively.

They made it through the forest to their destination without hearing so much as a single monster roar.

Leaves danced on the wind at the clearing's center. At the back was a single stump, maybe measuring a yard across.

"The boss should spawn any second."

"The what?! Oh, okay!"

Maple hastily drew her short sword and raised her great shield.

As she did, a green light appeared above the stump, quickly taking shape. Stepping out of the light was a creature that looked like a man made of wood.

The monster was on the small side, less than five and a half feet. It wore a hat made of vines and leaves.

In one hand, it held a simple wooden staff that had a flowering vine woven around the shaft.

Before either could attack, the creature waved the staff. Leaves swirled upward and toward them.

Pain moved swiftly, circling around the leaf swarm and landing a powerful hit on the boss. Maple did nothing of the kind.

Even armed with prior knowledge, she simply wasn't fast enough to dodge.

"Eep!"

The leaves surrounded her.

Anyone affected by this ability was forced to swap their current equipment with random gear from their inventory, locking those selections in until combat ended.

"......Uh?"

When the leaves vanished and Maple opened her eyes, she found herself in white armor.

Unlike Pain, Maple didn't really haul that much gear around.

Her accessories were scrambled, and the crown she'd found in the jungle earlier was on her head, but the rest of it was simply her sub-equipment.

"Yeah, I'm all good!"

She drew her new short sword, caught up with Pain, and used her usual skill.

"Martyr's Devotion!"

Wind blades shot at Pain, but Maple soaked the damage. None of them hurt her; she simply canceled out the attacks completely.

And if Maple was serving as the shield, Pain could devote himself to swinging his blade.

Blond hair. Blue eyes.

Both clad in pure-white armor. Like brother and sister.

Protected by the blessing of devotion, the knight showed no mercy, his divine blade gleaming even as it sliced through the creature's limbs.

Few could match his damage output, and it slashed the boss's HP.

"This should be real quick!"

"Looks like! Look at it go!"

Pain rained down more blows.

The boss raised wooden walls and summoned vine armor, but he hacked at them until they fell away.

And Maple's tanking never once faltered.

The boss's wind blades and leaf tornadoes both bounced right off her impotently.

This boss never stood a chance against this duo.

Its wooden body withered away before crumbling completely.

Pain immediately checked the new skill they got while Maple fixed her gear.

Green's Grace

10% boost to MP recovery speed.

Maple had sacrificed some HP to activate Martyr's Devotion, so she took a potion out of her inventory...and then finally remembered.

"Augh! I can't heal!"

*　　*　　*

She'd just used the skill out of habit.

Pain watched Maple flail around, wailing aloud.

Thinking that if he'd only seen her like this, he'd have been certain victory was his.

◆□◆□◆□◆□◆

Since Maple had accidentally destroyed her HP bar during the boss fight, she decided to leave Pain and the jungle behind.

With her HP this low, a single piercing attack would be the end of her.

And in the jungle, combat was a fairly common occurrence... it had already worn her out quite a bit.

She told him her plans and thanked him for his help.

"This was a valuable experience," he said. "I'd be honored to work with you again."

"Good luck!"

"Same to you."

Maple waved and vanished in a puff of light, returning to the regular map.

CHAPTER 11

Defense Build and the Rendezvous

"Where to next?" Pain muttered, on his own. "At least I know exactly where I am. That makes it easier to plan."

Most of the jungle looked completely the same, and this tree was one of the few discernible landmarks.

Pain decided to head to an area nearby where lots of golems spawned. That seemed like a good destination now that he'd gotten the skill he wanted.

He stepped onto the exit circle and was back on the twisted giant tree.

"Mm-hmm. Time to go."

Pain set out once more.

On his way down the stairs, he bumped into a party of four on their way up.

Chrome, Misery, Kanade, and Marx.

Both pairs had been heading for the same spot and met up not far from the tree, deciding to run the boss together.

They looked surprised to see Pain on his way down.

Chrome and Pain chatted a moment. When he heard where

Pain was headed, he conferred with his party and offered up a new proposal.

If Pain helped them out, they'd help him.

With this party, they needed someone who could dish out a lot of damage in a short amount of time.

"...Fair enough. Let's share info."

Accepting the offer, Pain told them everything he knew, making sure they would have everything they needed to win this fight.

Chrome asked a few questions, then concluded, "That works. We can handle this."

Pain's resources were still in good shape, and he'd already fought it once with Maple, allowing him to carefully observe its patterns from a position of safety.

Moreover, this eliminated any chance of failure.

"With the five of us, it won't take long."

Pain's prediction proved true.

He took the lead attack role, while Chrome used his shield to deflect the boss's blows.

With Pain relaxed and confident, he was able to handle this foe with maximum efficiency.

Chrome took no damage, easily soaking or deflecting everything the boss threw at them.

Pain and Marx found his performance reassuring—but perhaps not entirely because he was "strong" or "reliable."

Be that as it may, the other four all got the skill they had been searching for.

And once they were all back at the tree, they set out in search of golems.

*　　*　　*

They stayed close together.

This party was heavy on back-liners, so they couldn't exactly surge forward carelessly. They had to take their time, staying hidden.

Pain told Chrome that if they'd met up a few minutes earlier, they'd have had Maple along.

"She was here?"

"I was playing with her just before I found you. She's something else. Always has been."

"Never fought her myself. I'd like to give it a shot someday, but...that could get ugly."

Chrome had been playing with Maple for a while. (Though not as long as Sally.)

That meant he'd had time to think about how he could use his shield and skills against her attacks.

Whether that would lead to victory was another matter.

Chrome was confident he could survive her onslaught but didn't have anything that granted him a win condition.

"If the chance comes along, I'll go all out. I can be pretty tenacious," he said, thumping his chest.

"The way she is now... I'm not too far off from being able to cut her down."

"That's the spirit! But she has a tendency to evolve in the weirdest ways, so there's no guarantee she'll stay like this."

Chrome had seen it firsthand.

Maple would get stuck for ages, then suddenly grow explosively.

And nobody could tell when that cycle would come around—not even Maple herself.

"Heads up, golem time! Battle stations!"

Watching their surroundings as they talked, they made it to their destination—the golem-infested area.

Lots of moss-covered ruins here—more fallen pillars and rubble than there were trees.

Misery cast buffs on Pain and Chrome.

"Hmm, I haven't done much…better set some traps."

Marx switched from his on-the-go setup to instead ready some costlier traps that worked well against large foes.

While he was preparing those, Pain started hacking away at a golem's rock arms.

"A single golem is no challenge!"

He twisted himself to avoid its swing, then used Leap to strike at its torso.

To Pain, one golem no longer even required blocking.

This golem had been several times his height, yet Pain handily took it down all on his own.

The fight lasted less than a minute.

As he sheathed his blade, Chrome came over.

"Uh, Pain… Look there."

"Hmm? Interesting."

Where Chrome pointed…

Shattered pillars. Moss-covered ruins.

…And a golem emerging from the shadows. Not just one, either. Golem after golem marched out, rocky feet thudding as they approached.

As if they were intent on preventing anyone from heading farther in.

The party watched as the area filled with golems, like gray ink blotting out the landscape.

"Pain, what do we do?"

"Take out the bare minimum and make our getaway!"

"Got it."

With that brief exchange, Chrome and Pain readied their weapons.

Misery cast an AGI buff on everyone in preparation for their imminent escape.

"Both sides'll be held up briefly by traps, but not for long."

"Let me use a grimoire... Hmm, do I have anything that has piercing? This one?"

Kanade pulled out a yellow-green tome.

Just before battle began, the tome glowed, activating.

Winds roared overhead.

The howling gale grew in volume, taking direction, sweeping onward.

Loud as any explosion.

Spears made of air suddenly impaled a number of golems.

Dirt flew, and the ground beneath their feet shook.

"It doesn't do as much damage as it might seem to at a glance," Kanade said. "Hurry!"

At his urging, Pain led them through a gap in the golem formation.

"Don't...you move..."

There was a burst of light beneath the feet of the golems on each side, impeding their movements.

Marx was burning through MP fast, but Misery quickly used her skills to top him up.

She could help people recover more than just health.

There were limits to it—it was hardly infinite—but it was enough to get them out of this jam.

"There's too many! Don't even try and fight!" Chrome bellowed, deflecting a fist to the side so it hit the ground.

Breaking free of this ambush was hard enough already; trying to take on the golems in a stand-up fight would be downright suicidal.

But just as they seemed trapped—

—a burst of fire decapitated a golem nearby.

◆□◆□◆□◆□◆

Why had a golem suddenly gone up in flames, crumbling into a shower of light?

Pain and Chrome spun toward it, baffled. But the flames weren't finished yet; they were already assaulting the next golem at the direction of a lone girl—Mii.

She, too, had found herself surrounded by golems—and the combined spawns that had been triggered were what resulted in the ridiculous numbers they were facing now.

Mii had heard them fighting and naturally moved in their direction. Kanade, Chrome, and Pain all had gear that was recognizable at a distance, and the other two were friends of hers, so she immediately recognized them.

"If they're all here, then…"

She generated a massive pillar of fire beneath the golems' feet. It caught both the golems around her and some around the other group.

This alone wasn't enough to kill them, but they did *stagger*.

And that gave the other party enough opening to rush over to Mii's position.

Misery and Marx suggested they were better off joining forces.

Mii took one look at them and called out, "Misery!"

"On it!"

Misery knew exactly what Mii wanted.

She started channeling over her excess MP.

"Ready...!"

The name of the skill was drowned out by the tramping of golem feet, but what happened next made it clear this skill was *insanely* powerful.

A wall of fire sprang up around them, creating a straight corridor through the golem horde.

"Clandestine Bloom," Marx whispered.

Slender tendrils grew around each of the players, and white flowers blossomed.

This skill could only be activated when out of sight of monsters. The cost was rather high, but it kept them from spotting you for thirty seconds.

When the effect wore off, the flowers withered and fell, making it hard to miss.

"The golems despawn quick if they lose track of you," Mii said.

She started walking down the path of fire.

"Follow her. These walls won't stay up for long," Misery said. Then she caught up with Mii, whispering, "Mind if we join you?"

"Please do. Dealing with them alone was...a *lot*."

Once Maple had uncovered her secret, it hadn't taken Mii long to mess up in front of Misery. Now two people knew she was just role-playing.

But being able to drop the act around Misery meant she could relax more in her Guild Home.

Misery took Mii's words and translated them for the others.

"Mii has agreed to a temporary alliance. Our forces are now one!"

And Misery was perfectly willing to help maintain Mii's painstakingly cultivated image.

"My attack magic is all over the place right now, so that's a relief," Kanade said.

Only Misery saw how relieved Mii looked.

"Then let's keep moving. This stuff is time limited, right?" Chrome said, waving everyone on.

And thus, they escaped the golem ambush before the flowers wore off.

Once again, Mii was relieved that the jungle was designed to *not* catch fire.

They moved on together.

"That's gotta be it."

Once past the golem blockade, the next thing they saw was naturally what the golems were protecting.

Pain was pointing at some ruins made of moss-covered rock.

And deep within those ruins was a larger building—the kind that clearly had *something* inside.

There were no monsters around, so they made it to the building without further trouble.

They found a long, long set of staircases that led deep underground.

This was clearly the way to go, so down they went.

Their goal was the treasure that obviously lay hidden below—whatever it might be.

The stairs had no illumination at all.

And they had to make several turns. Soon, the light from above was not enough.

"I've got a lantern," Misery offered, pulling one from her inventory.

With that, they had enough light to see again.

"Nothing on the stairs," Chrome said, peering over his shield. Nothing here but endless walls.

"......! I can see something up ahead. I think?"

"Mii?" Misery said, glancing her way.

Mii looked shifty immediately. She was getting way too used to being herself around Misery.

"Yes, I see it clearly now. The stairs end not much farther on. At a door. I trust you all know what that means."

Mii's eyes were glowing red.

This was a night vision skill that let her see farther than everyone else.

It wasn't long before the others could see the door, too. It was made of stone, with only a groove cut in it—a handhold to help slide it open.

Chrome got a good grip and tried to do just that.

"Hmm? No use. It won't budge."

"Must require a certain Strength threshold. In which case, allow me."

Pain put his sword away and gave the door a heave.

There was a grinding sound as the door slowly slid open.

Blinding light poured out.

Corridors and stairs ran up, down, left, and right.

Magic circles glittered here and there alongside ancient switches that seemed clearly significant in some way.

This was a *true* labyrinth. A real dungeon. They paused for a moment, gaping at the view that had just opened up before them.

"Uh...so where do we start?" Chrome said.

"Too many choices," Pain grumbled. "I don't like it."

On his left alone there were five or six magic circles.

This could take forever.

"What now...? Where should we even go...?"

The look on Marx's face was almost as bad as when he'd first laid eyes on Maple's Atrocity form.

Clearly, he was about ready to leave and was only staying put because they had *this* party together.

"I vote we proceed at random. Monsters won't be a threat. And thinking about it won't get us anywhere."

"Good point, Mii. I suggest we start by tapping a circle or that lever."

"I can keep track of what paths we take. At the least, we won't get lost or forget where we've been."

That settled their plan for the moment.

There was a switch nearby, so they decided to pull it and see what happened.

"Here goes nothing!" Chrome said. He glanced back once with his hands on the shaft. Everyone nodded. He hauled the shaft to the other side.

As he did, the network of staircases all rearranged themselves. Walls opened up, revealing new corridors, while previously existing passages vanished from view.

Some magic circles faded, and new ones began to glow.

A single switch had transformed the entire maze.

"Wowza..."

Marx was now at full Maple/Atrocity face.

Chrome looked pretty grim himself.

"What now, Pain? You can pick what we should try next, if you want."

"Honestly, it seems like a giant headache. Ha-ha-ha. Chrome, the choice is yours."

With the two front-liners trying to foist the burden of making a decision off onto each other, Kanade spoke up.

"Almost every staircase, passage, and magic circle changed—but there is one corridor that didn't. Should we try that one?"

Kanade had a flawless recollection of the previous layout.

What no one else here could notice, his eyes immediately spotted.

"Another impossibly unique skill...," Marx muttered.

"Definitely more the Sally type," Misery agreed.

No one objected to the proposal, so everyone followed Kanade. The passage led to a similar room with another switch.

"If it just keeps doing this...most of these must be traps."

"Kanade, this is all you."

"Trust me on this one!"

On they went.

Slipping safely past horrifying beasts and deadly traps.

All the malice poured into this dungeon's design was defeated by a single player—Kanade.

Every clever trick designed to protect what lay within was foiled by an even cleverer mind.

After a long trek from maze to maze, they found themselves in a room that was like none before.

Resting at the back was a coffin, decorated with gold and jewels. The room was otherwise empty. Just a floor of sand and dry stones. Nothing out of the ordinary there.

But the coffin on the floor was a good five yards tall, and nobody here assumed it had treasure inside.

Their actual assumption proved true.

As they approached, there was a scraping sound as the lid slid open.

From within emerged a head decorated with a glittering crown. A skeletal king, wielding a golden scepter.

And where its eyes should be, there were instead dark fires that served only to emphasize the hollow pits.

"Here it comes! Brace yourselves!" Pain yelled.

And the battle with the skeletal king began.

◆□◆□◆□◆□◆

As the battle started, Pain and Mii both hurled themselves at the boss.

Chrome made to chase after them, but the tip of the scepter lit up with blue fire.

And the seemingly ordinary floor split open, weapons thrusting upward, skeletons emerging.

Black goo dripped from their rusty spears and swords.

"Chrome, hold the line in the rear!" Pain yelled, slicing down any skeletons that got in his way.

"Roger! Taunt!"

Chrome turned on a dime, keeping his shield close to the three back-liners. The room was filled with skeletons, and it would be a fatal mistake to let them swarm their party's mages.

And as Chrome stabilized his defense of the rear, the back line let loose with roaring fires and howling winds overhead.

Kanade was using grimoires with broad AOE spells while Misery was using similar innate spells.

Marx was focused on backing up Chrome, trapping skeletons to ease the pressure on him.

But using Taunt assured there were a *lot* of skeletons focusing on him.

Chrome was using every shield trick in the book to keep them back, hacking away with his cleaver the whole while, but in time, a spear found its mark.

He reacted quickly, knocking the assailant away with his shield, but red sparks sprayed from his arm.

"Not much damage from the hit, but…crap! Bad news! Look out, everyone, these skeletons can inflict damage-over-time effects!"

Chrome's health bar was steadily dropping.

The effect only lasted a few seconds, but clearly, poison wasn't responsible—which meant there were no possible countermeasures.

"And the skeleton mobs seem like they have infinite spawns!"

"In that case…focus your attacks around Mii and Pain. I'll lay traps here."

Marx pulled crystals and some type of seed from the pouches on his waist, scattering them around.

The crystals shattered, and several nearby skeletons were bound by crackling light.

Those seeds grew fast, forming a hefty vine barrier and blocking the enemy's approach.

This left Kanade and Misery free to focus their fire on the front line.

The closer Pain and Mii got to the boss, the more skeletons had stood in their way, but the powerful cover fire finally let them get in range.

"Does fire work?"

Mii waved an arm, and Flame Empress's fire balls struck the boss, taking a visible chunk of its HP bar.

But even as its health dropped, the resulting red sparks were drowned out by a pitch-black fluid.

Mii managed to avoid a direct hit, but several ancillary drops struck her.

"A DOT effect…!"

One of the worst effects to encounter in a no-heal zone.

"But it's made of paper. Holy Condemnation!"

Pain swung his sword, and the boss raised the scepter to block it. He parried that and made a deep gouging cut upward from flesh-less chest to skull.

Tanking his share of black goop, Pain attempted another strike, but more black fluid started flowing over the coffin's brim.

"Tch. Mii!"

"One more!"

Mii smacked the boss's head again, making it stagger, and then she and Pain leaped back.

There were skeletons where they landed, but the constant spell barrage from the rear took care of those. They were free to focus on the boss.

The coffin fluid coated the floor around the boss and stopped.

Approaching on foot guaranteed they'd take some damage.

Then the boss flung the scepter upward. The ceiling absorbed it.

And all the boss's bones began to gleam with a dark brilliance.

As they did, half the mob skeletons crumpled and vanished, but black goo began dropping from the ceiling.

And each drop carved a bit of HP away.

"Everyone forward! All-out attack!" Pain roared, charging in.

The back line surged forward to mid-range—where their attacks could reach the boss itself.

But the boss's insidious glow grew brighter still, reducing the effectiveness of their attacks.

"Chrome, can you get next to it? It's got a strong buff…but I can dispel that," Marx said.

There was a white disc over his right eye, like a monocle.

This allowed him to observe the boss's stats in detail.

"Will you two be okay?"

"I'll use a defensive grimoire. Don't worry."

The confidence in Kanade's voice gave Chrome the final push he needed. He took Marx under his wing, and they plunged through the skeleton horde together.

He took plenty of damage, but Marx made it to his destination.

"All right...Holy Chains!"

A number of yellow circles appeared around the boss, from which emerged gleaming white chains. These wrapped around the skeleton king.

The boss's black gleam vanished, and as a bonus, it was immobilized for three full seconds.

And with Mii and Pain around, those three seconds were costly.

"Finish it!"

"Way ahead of you!"

Mii's fireballs scorched the bones, and a pillar of fire burned it and its coffin together.

Pain's holy combo carved a deep cross in the boss's face.

The black drops had everyone below half health—but at last, the skeleton king returned to its eternal slumber.

After the boss's death light faded, the coffin alone remained.

When they peered inside, they found six scrolls and six silver medals, arranged like they'd been buried with the ghastly king.

There were also a few rusty swords, but the scrolls and medals were the only things that could be claimed as items.

Each took their share and checked the scroll's skill.

Reaper's Mire

For thirty seconds after use, attacks apply additional piercing damage equal to a quarter of the damage dealt. Five-minute cooldown.

This sounded a lot like the black goop that had done a number on all their HP bars.

Each of them considered how to best incorporate it into their builds.

Several of them found it merely interesting, while others looked immensely pleased.

Not long after, they left the dungeon behind and explored the jungle until their HP finally ran out.

Defense Build and the King of Light

A few days after their party cleared the jungle ruins...

Maple was sprawled out on the couch in her Guild Home.

"Augh..."

Leaving the jungle when her HP ran low was one thing, but she wasn't having any luck finding the item she needed to go back.

And the more she looked, the less she cared. This left her feeling alone and sorry for herself while all her friends ran around the jungle.

"Who cares about that dumb jungle?! I had a good run! A real adventure!"

She jumped to her feet, cast her sinking mood aside, and decided to go out.

And not in search for more jungle tickets.

"Where have I *not* been...? Oh!"

A light bulb went off, and she headed back onto the cloud field, taking her sweet time.

"Wow, so pretty!"

Before Maple's eyes was the cloudy field where lightning struck ceaselessly.

Chrome had told her about this, and with nothing better to do, she'd come to check it out.

"Welp, let's give it a shot!"

All fired up, she sallied forth into the maelstrom.

With thunder rumbling all around, the inevitable soon happened: A bolt of lightning landed right on top of her.

"Eep! Oh. Nice! Didn't hurt a bit."

Mere lightning was not enough to budge Maple's HP.

And naturally, nothing could paralyze her.

"Guess I'll keep going!"

She headed farther in. Dozens of lightning bolts struck her, but she remained impervious.

"I wonder if I could dodge them like Sally does? Whoa! Nope, definitely can't."

She'd tried hopping around a bit, and a bolt had gone right through her. This startled her enough that she decided to stop trying.

"Whatever, see if I...whah!"

She gave it one last shot, and the lightning storm clearly decided to punish her for it. This time, she really did give up.

"Okay, just walking. Walking away!"

Maple might have changed her mind, but not her stats. Lightning kept bouncing off her as she trudged along. Eventually, she reached the end of the thunderstorm zone and saw a beautiful white sea of clouds ahead.

"Did I get through? I hope there's something here!"

She looked around, venturing deeper into the calm area.

It didn't take her long to spot something standing on the clouds.

It looked to be about five times her height. She squinted at it.

"Um...is it some sort of chair?"

It was as white as the clouds beneath it, but shinier.

And more of a throne than a chair.

It reacted to her approach, white light coalescing above it.

The dazzling shape eventually solidified into a humanoid figure big enough to sit on the massive throne.

There was a crown resting upon his head and whiskers made from light upon his wizened face.

The luxurious garments resting upon his frame were fit for any king.

Magic circles appeared around His Majesty, bathing the whole area around the throne in white light.

Clearly, diplomacy was not an option.

The magic circles began firing arrows of light at Maple.

"Cool. Atrocity!"

The arrows bounced right off Maple's monstrous skin.

"Chaaaarge!"

Maple broke into a run.

But when she neared the gleaming circle of light, her tough exterior melted away.

"Huh?! Augh!"

She fell out of it and went rolling across the ground.

When she finally got up, she looked around, wondering what had happened.

The arrows were still peppering her, and the king was most definitely still on his throne.

"Well... Hydra!"

She held up her sword, but no poison responded to her call.

"That's weird. Predators! Saturating Chaos! Full Deploy!"

She ran down her list of skills. She was able to deploy her weapons, but everything else failed.

The ground around her was glowing.

This was hallowed ground, a place where evil skills were sealed and unusable.

And Maple's skills mostly leaned a bit too evil for the King of Light.

"Commence Assault!"

Bullets, cannon shells, and lasers all opened fire, but the arrows of light outnumbered them, and very few got through.

And when they did, they did no damage.

Maple's artillery fire was less focused on individual power than quantity of hits, so they didn't really work on anything truly tanky.

And since their strength was a set value, their usefulness was going to decline the further she got in the game.

"Hmm...what now? It can't hurt me, but Devour doesn't work..."

She'd seen an arrow hit her shield like it was *just* a normal shield and was starting to feel discouraged.

It couldn't beat her, but she couldn't beat it.

Both of them were just raining ranged attacks on each other and getting nowhere fast.

"Maybe I should get closer."

Arrows bouncing off every inch of her, she approached the king and his throne.

And as she reached his feet...

"Yeah...attacking doesn't work."

She poked his feet with her sword, but naturally, this was useless.

She smacked him with her shield and called out Syrup, trying its attacks—all to no avail.

Maple stood there for a few more minutes, then clapped her hands once and turned around.

"Retreat! Retreeeeat!"

Deciding she had no chance, she just let the arrows bounce off her back and headed back through the lightning field once more.

When she returned to the main field, she paused, considering her options.

"Is there really nothing else I can do? Hmm... Oh, right. I heard some rumors in town. I've just gotta track that down!"

With this in mind, she hopped on Syrup and flew back to town.

"There was that row of shops, so let's start there."

She checked her cash on hand and got off Syrup just outside of town.

"Let's see, let's see... I know they had it on the first stratum..."

She checked each shop, scoping out their selection.

And after an hour of shopping...

She used a great deal of her money buying a whole slew of items.

"Cool. I bought a lot! Not sure all of these will help, but...let's try again tomorrow!"

She scrolled down her inventory once more and logged out. It was time to go back to the real world.

AFTERWORD

I know I always say this, but once again, let me start by thanking everyone who's read the series this far. And if you've happened to get curious and picked this up, I hope you take this opportunity to read it for yourself.

Hello! I am Yuumikan.

We're already at Volume 5 of *I Don't Want to Get Hurt, so I'll Max Out My Defense*. But I suppose it's been more than a year since the first volume released.

Since the print release began, they've made commercials and started a manga adaption, and the year seemed to go by just like *that*.

But my attitude hasn't changed. I'm always trying to bring my readers a better book...and better news.

And with the one-year anniversary, I have some *very* good news!

Bofuri is getting an anime!

*　　*　　*

A year ago, I would never have believed this. It's possible I still don't. But this would never have happened without your support. Thank you so much!

This is an opportunity to show everyone how great Maple and company are, and I hope it helps repay the great debt I owe you all. I have no idea how else I would even begin to do it. Perhaps it's just one little thing after another.

So with that good news, *I Don't Want to Get Hurt, so I'll Max Out My Defense*, Vol. 5 draws to a close.

My thanks to everyone who has opened doors for me.
Praying that I may have more good news to come.
And looking forward to seeing you all in Volume 6!

Yuumikan

The Detective Is Already Dead

When the story begins without its hero

Kimihiko Kimizuka has always been a magnet for trouble and intrigue. For as long as he can remember, he's been stumbling across murder scenes or receiving mysterious attaché cases to transport. When he met Siesta, a brilliant detective fighting a secret war against an organization of pseudohumans, he couldn't resist the call to become her assistant and join her on an epic journey across the world.

...Until a year ago, that is. Now he's returned to a relatively normal and tepid life, knowing the adventure must be over. After all, the detective is already dead.

Volume 1 available wherever books are sold!

YenPress.com

TANTEI HA MO, SHINDEIRU. Vol. 1
©nigozyu 2019
Illustration: Umibouzu
KADOKAWA CORPORATION